'I see no point in hanging about here,' Louise retorted swiftly, feeling her anger rise again. 'It's quite obvious that you're enjoying this cat-and-mouse game, but I'm not!'

'Believe me, Miss Holden, this is no game—it's deadly serious. Maybe I've underestimated your grasp of the situation.'

She met the icy gaze unflinchingly. 'Let me assure you, I stick to what I said last night about refusing to discuss my personal affairs. I believe I'm well qualified to do the job that was offered me, and I'd be fully prepared to take whatever comes under difficult circumstances. Other than that, my life is my own, and I do not intend my confidential relationships to become an appendix to my CV!' She stood up, holding out her hand. 'Now perhaps you'll let me have my papers and I'll take up no more of your time.'

'Sit down, Miss Holden!' Piers Morell roared.

The command was so totally unexpected she obeyed immediately.

Frances Crowne's nursing career was set aside for marriage and three children, yet left a sense of thwarted ambition. Later a secretarial career at an agricultural college was followed by free-lance writing of romantic fiction and articles for women's magazines. A chance remark at a party led to her writing her first Medical Romance. Woven now with romance her nursing ties have come full circle in a most gratifying way.

Previous Titles

INSTANT CARE
DESERT DOCTOR
DANGEROUS SYMPTOMS

LOVE'S CASUALTIES

BY

FRANCES CROWNE

MILLS & BOON LIMITED
ETON HOUSE   18–24 PARADISE ROAD
RICHMOND   SURREY   TW9 1SR

*First published in Great Britain 1990
by Mills & Boon Limited*

© Frances Crowne 1990

*Australian copyright 1990
Philippine copyright 1990
This edition 1990*

ISBN 0 263 76885 6

*Set in 10 on 10½ pt Linotron Plantin
03-9007-58368
Typeset in Great Britain by Centracet, Cambridge
Made and printed in Great Britain*

CHAPTER ONE

THE wedding veil drifted across her face. Radiant in white brocade, Louise entered the church, pausing excitedly before gripping her father's arm and walking up the aisle to where Raymond would be waiting. . .

Raucous laughter greeted her. From relatives, friends, the vicar, the noise rose to a deafening crescendo as distorted faces swung across her vision, the taunting chorus of 'We told you so. . .we told you so. . .' making her cry out aloud in anguish. . .

Breathless, and gasping her way back to blessed wakefulness, Louise Holden emerged with relief from the recurring nightmare of the past year, one that left her weak and trembling in every limb. She sat up in bed, pushing back the long fair hair from her face, her troubled eyes dazed as she drew in several deep breaths to still the frantic beating of her heart.

'*Ma chère*—are you all right?' Monique Lefarge, with whom she shared a room, was looking down at her anxiously. 'What is wrong? Why do you cry out in your sleep so? It is the second time in two days! You must calm yourself, otherwise the trip will be impossible for you!' Her worried face with its frame of short dark hair stared at Louise, whom she'd known for such a short time, yet with whom she had shared such an instant rapport. 'Can I be of some 'elp to you?'

'No, I'm OK, thanks, Monique—honestly,' Louise said quickly. Although she was still preoccupied, her grey-green eyes were already regaining their usual bright lustre. She took a drink of water from her bedside table, giving her new friend a quick smile. 'I. . .tend to have nightmares occasionally, if I'm in a strange bed, perhaps. It's nothing. . .' She replaced the glass with, she hoped, a steady hand. 'Probably also the heat—it takes a bit of getting used to.'

'You are right. Dean's 'otel is not the best, but thank God for air-conditioning.' Monique stood up, looking out of the window, glancing at the dawn light and a pink glow that suffused the mountain peaks across the border between Pakistan and Afghanistan. 'But do you think you are wise, coming 'ere to Peshawar,' she persisted gently, 'when your nerves are. . .are. . .' her black, expressive eyebrows shot up beneath a thick, straight fringe, her narrow shoulders shrugged, '. . .so in splinters?'

Louise was rapidly recovering herself as the girl turned away from the window. 'There's nothing wrong, Monique, I assure you. Nerves of iron, that's me! Maybe I'm a trifle edgy about our getting under way. If that's the case, the sooner our boss, the world-famed Piers Morell, turns up, the better!'

Monique gave a long, supple stretch, murmuring, '*D'accord*,' then proceeded to indulge in some very tricky exercises while Louise looked on with undisguised admiration. 'But that man will take 'is time!' Monique declared eventually, leaping to her feet and squatting cross-legged at the foot of her bed. 'I 'ave not lived in Paris without 'earing many things about this Adonis with the face of a saint and a 'eart of steel.'

Louise slid a silk dressing-gown over her nakedness. 'He's only a man, Monique. I don't give a damn what he's like, so long as he does the job he's renowned for.'

Monique's eyes flashed intuitively. 'You do not like men, per'aps?'

Louise scooped up her sponge bag and towel and headed for the shower. 'Let's say that as far as I'm concerned they're a very much overrated species!' She threw the words casually over her shoulder with a laugh, minutes later sending the ice-cold needles of water stabbing at her tall, slender body. Closing her eyes, she hoped she could keep up this brittle, devil-take-the-hindmost attitude she had painfully built up around herself—particularly through the six months to come, when she would be putting herself to an even greater test of physical endurance—that of self-preservation.

Back in the bedroom, Monique had not been idle. She was busily pouring cups of tea for them both from a very old-fashioned earthenware teapot. 'I managed to get them to understand in the kitchen that we needed some English tea, et voilà!' She grinned, glancing at Louise. 'You will 'ave some?'

'Please. You're a marvel, Monique, I don't know how you managed it!' She sipped the pale golden liquid as the other girl watched anxiously. 'Mmm, perfect!'

'Bon. Now we must 'urry before we are late at the 'ospital.'

The hospital was little more than a grouping of wooden constructions used as a part clearing station for the constant stream of casualties that flowed in from the war zone, mostly with gunshot wounds received by design or accident. Monique, a well-qualified nursing sister and physiotherapist, was working with Louise, who at the age of twenty-six had completed her training as an MD—apart from beginning to specialise in surgery—while acting as one of several housemen at a famous hospital in the heart of London, and had had little chance to put her skills into practise. Raymond, an ambitiously rising young barrister, had also needed a lot of her time. Or so he'd insisted. She switched her mind back to the gaping leg wound she had just sutured.

'OK, Monique, I think he'll be all right; the site's clean enough.'

The patient was removed from the small room, which was cramped and ill-equipped. Just then the door burst open unexpectedly and packets of sterile dressings from America tumbled down all over the floor.

'Ooops—sorry, girls!'

Monique raised her eyebrows at Louise, saying patiently, 'This is Dr Alain Savarin, Louise.'

Louise smiled. 'Hello, Alain, glad you—er—dropped in!'

The round-faced man with sparse fair hair and a big smile shot a hand out to Louise in welcome as he scrambled up off the floor after retrieving the packages. 'Everything happens to me!' He grinned goodnaturedly. 'Good to see you, anyway.' His keen brown eyes surveyed her through gold-rimmed spectacles. 'My apologies for not making it before, but when the first of our group began to arrive earlier this week, we were immediately press-ganged to start work, no chance at all for getting to know each other. Isn't that so, Monique?'

Monique turned from stowing the packets. 'Yes, it is right, we 'ave been very busy.'

Louise was adjusting her mask. 'Are there any more to do out there?' she asked Monique.

'Just two minor ones. Shall I bring them in?'

Before Louise could answer, Alain said brightly, 'Well, I'll be off. I have a patient to see first, then we'll all go back for lunch together.' He threw a glance at Louise, who was reading through the next casualty's notes. 'You must meet Jan Svensen also, Louise—a fine fellow from Sweden.' He smiled as he went through the door.

Once the two remaining patients had been attended to, and placed in the care of the grossly overworked local nurses, Monique and Louise walked back to the hotel with Alain, only too conscious of the rapidly forming collection of fresh casualties already waiting for when they returned that afternoon in the still blistering heat. At the end of a dusty, tree-lined avenue they crossed spongy green lawns to the tin-roofed, single-storeyed building which was to be 'home' until they left for their ultimate destination.

Jan Svensen had been looking out for them in the small reception area, Alain having suggested he sleep on that morning after a rather turbulent air trip on his way out to Pakistan. But Louise thought she had never seen such a fit-looking specimen. Alain, thick-set and of medium height, introduced them. 'This is Jan, Louise, our male nurse and journalist. Dr Louise Holden, Jan.'

Louise murmured a greeting as the man, about the same age as herself, gripped her hand, dark blue eyes smiling and enhancing his Scandinavian blondness and tall, athletic build. 'Pleasure, Louise. An attractive doctor indeed!' he smiled disarmingly. 'Alain, remind me to make certain that you are unavoidably detained when I'm in need of medical attention!'

Louise joined in the laughter as they went into the rather gloomy dining-room with its drab-coloured walls. Jan Svensen seemed nice, she thought as they began the meal; his light, easy manner and mildly flirtatious banter was just what they needed to balance Alain's kindly but very slightly pompous attitude. The Frenchman's constant smile too could be a little wearing. . .But quickly she threw off these first impressions, amazed at how easily she'd been absorbed into this circle of people who, one bright morning in April less than a week ago, had been virtual strangers to her. At the interview with the Médicins Sans Frontières in Paris, names of people in the group with whom she would travel had been mentioned but they had meant nothing to her. All that had mattered was that at last she'd been offered a job which would blot out the past most terrible year of her whole life, and that had been the only thing she had been concerned about.

Later, drinking coffee on the veranda, Alain started up a desultory conversation about Piers Morell. 'You have not yet met him, then, Louise?'

'Not so far as I know.'

Alain chuckled. 'He is not the sort of man easily forgotten if you had! A strict disciplinarian and a man of strength.' He laughed heartily. 'On second thoughts, perhaps I should rephrase that! He expects a great deal from the people who take part in these trips. He himself is very well travelled and understands the need for the right types. I believe he thinks nothing of refusing to take a journalist or doctor if at the final meeting he feels they are unsuitable, despite all the careful vetting by the interviewers in Paris.'

Louise pushed her coffee-cup to one side. 'So, it seems I am the only one not yet finally vetted by him?'

Monique glanced across the table. 'Do not let it worry you, Louise. Although we all got on well enough with 'im, no one really knows what makes Piers Morell—'ow do you say?—tick! Alain is teasing you, I think!'

Alain looked slightly put out at Monique's words, although he was still smiling. 'No, Monique, I am not, I am not! But you must all make up your own minds about Mr Morell. As far as I am concerned such an illustrious Fellow of the Royal College of Surgeons demands our respect and admiration if we are to succeed in our mission.'

Monique admonished him with her elfin smile. 'We would not dream of doing otherwise, *monsieur*!'

Jan Svensen was nevertheless looking impatient. 'But when are we likely to expect the man?' he asked, his English tinged only faintly with the melodic lilt of his own language. 'Knowing him, I would have thought he'd have given an exact time of arrival.'

Alain threw his hands up in the air. '*Mon Dieu*, the impatience of youth! But to answer your question, Jan— any time now, I imagine. Piers has had much to arrange—medical supplies, horses and many other travel details. As you know, we shall be crossing the border in the company of the Mujahedin rebels, or the resistance as they prefer to be called, so Piers will be organising things at their offices here. But we are in safe hands—he knows his way about this part of the world. And of course he's fluent in Persian—Farsi, as it's known in Afghanistan.'

There was little time for Alain to say much more. The

lunch hour had flown and they were due back at the hospital to give what help they could to the beleaguered staff. For the rest of the sultry, airless afternoon, while she worked, Louise reflected upon what she'd heard of Piers Morell, the man. He certainly sounded the right type for the job, that of leading a team into potentially dangerous territory, thereafter supervising relief of staff already working at the mountain clinic, and preparing to hand over to the villagers now that hostilities were reputedly at an end.

A slight *frisson* of fear went through her—not at the thought of what lay ahead so much as her initial encounter with the man who seemed to have made such varied impressions on the rest of the party. That being so, outwardly to her colleagues—even Piers Morell—she would be good at her job, as her recent exams had proved, but submit to nothing with which she did not fully agree. Mr Piers Morell could accept her as she was, or do the other thing!

Brave words indeed, she thought wryly, a few hours later that evening when just after dinner the man himself joined them on the veranda for coffee. Louise had taken little notice of a tall, distinguished-looking man, perhaps mid-thirties, crossing the lawn, wearing a stone-coloured tropical suit, the sort that costs the earth in order for the wearer to appear relaxed and unobtrusively elegant. Nevertheless, it was something of a surprise when he strolled casually towards them.

But when greetings were exchanged, and he was being introduced to her by a slightly fluttered Alain, the actual manifestation of the man at last came as a slight shock to Louise. It was not the good-looking physical features so much as the. . .almost majestically arrogant presence. When he took her hand, she saw only a burning intensity of purpose in the long-lashed eyes, black as night, yet bright as dawn. They mesmerised her as he spoke, the firm lips curving into a reserved smile.

'Dr Holden—Louise. . .how very nice that we meet

at last. I trust you had a good journey out here, and the rest of our party have looked after you?'

'Extremely well, thank you,' she said after shaking hands, very conscious of his scrutiny. 'Everyone has been most kind.'

He nodded approval, then made sure each of them was comfortably seated before embarking upon the words he knew they were waiting to hear. Louise, meanwhile, studied the man's high cheekbones, long, angular jaw and square chin, the deeply tanned face already showing signs of a faintly shadowy stubble on the fine complexion. Was he all the things that had been hinted at?

From her expression at the other end of the table, even Monique looked as if she were still weighing up her thoughts on the man against the gossip she had heard in Paris. However, once Piers Morell began to speak, Louise soon forgot such speculation as she listened to the deep, authoritative voice, rich in tone and calmly persuasive while outlining what lay before them. A long, well-shaped hand occasionally pushed back a thick strand of straight dark hair; hair that seemed to have a life of its own and curled defiantly behind his ears and just above his collar. He sifted a sheaf of papers in front of him, head bent, dark, sleek eyebrows knitted in concentration. On looking up, he gave a small grin almost of conspiracy that swung to the side of his face, which immediately made them warm to him. 'I know you'll all be glad to hear that we are now ready for departure the day after tomorrow, Saturday, twelve midnight.' As if allowing time for his news to sink in, he took off his jacket, murmuring, 'To hell with formality.' He loosened his tie at the neck of his ivory silk shirt, only then appearing to relax; but not so much that he lost one speck of the charisma that seemed to emanate from him.

No doubt he knows this only too well, Louise mused uncharitably—just part of a big act. But grudgingly she had to admit he did have appeal, as he continued.

'I have now completed talks with the Mujaheddin. They drove a hard bargain, but that is because they need all the cash they can get their hands on for their cause. Still, I'm relieved to say we have reached satisfactory agreement on costs.'

The general murmur of approval around the table was the signal for Alain to call a waiter to bring in a tray of long, cool drinks. Piers was turning up his shirt-sleeves over mahogany-coloured forearms, an expensive gold wrist-watch flattening the soft dark hairs beneath the strap. He had the look of one expecting loyal and eager support from them all, and Louise concluded subconsciously that there was no doubt he would get it.

'Any questions so far?' He smiled, giving each of them a quizzical glance. 'No? Right, we'll carry on. The Mujaheddin, as you're aware, are very tough, therefore this will be no easy trip. I want to stress that, once we meet up with them, the Commander—Commander Anjum—will be in charge to give us safe passage. What he says goes. Tomorrow I want you all to get kitted out at the Khyber Bazaar in traditional dress so that you look a little less conspicuous. Monique and Louise will be Muslims, we men, Mujahedin. We'll be on the road with some two hundred rebels, eighty horses and mules, plus our own twenty or more animals carrying the invaluable medical supplies. . .' He paused. 'OK so far?'

'What about food?' Monique asked with determined practicality.

'Most will be arranged for us. Although we ourselves have a certain amount of dried milk, cereal, concentrated fruit juice, etcetera, this is mostly intended for babies and children at the clinic when we arrive. Nevertheless, if things became desperate we could make use of it. The Muj have their own methods of providing sustenance along the route.' He glanced at their rapt faces, the quizzical expressions, and his eyes smouldered with laughter. 'OK, I know—the next question, if I'm not mistaken, is the distance to be covered. Five hundred miles, to be precise—quite a walk to get to work! But seriously, we do have to rely on the rebels. Our diet in the main will be mostly goat, bread—or *nan* as it's called here—and rice. Chicken and fruit if we're lucky. I'll say no more than that!'

Again his strong smile encompassed them all, melting their hearts, it seemed. Louise sensed the feeling of collective relief that they were indeed in the presence of a born leader, whatever else she might have heard about him.

Alain, who had been silent until now, ran a hand ruminatively over his chin. 'What about the—er—realities, the danger?'

'Being smuggled over the border, you mean?' Piers said with delightful insouciance.

'Well. . .yes.'

'The aim is that we move mostly at night. Obviously it will not be possible all the time, but preferable when we can.'

'As a medical team with our own journalist, when exactly do we start our official duties, then?' Louise asked amid laughter. 'I mean, as soon as we set off on the journey?'

Piers gave her a brief grin, brushing contemplative fingers down his jaw. 'Now, enthusiasm is what I like to hear! Good question, Louise!'

She was annoyed to find herself blushing, quite sure it had nothing to do with the heat of the night or the rather potent 'fruit' drink she'd enjoyed. Piers Morell possessed that easy nonchalance that could so swiftly turn his perfectly valid comment into a risqué slant just for the benefit of his audience.

He was smiling, not at her, but he carried on with what he had to say, yet no doubt thinking she would be easy prey. He was in for a surprise when he realised that her 'enthusiasm' no longer included being dazzled by a good-looking man—rather the exact opposite. . .His words got through to her.

'A Land Rover will be taking us to a secret destination to join the Mujahedin, and will be painted to resemble an ambulance, for as you know foreign medics and press are the only people allowed to take such trips. Not that we're anything but authentic; it simply pays to be cautious at the border.' His eyes fastened on Louise. 'To answer your question more specifically, the moment we get into that ambulance on the night we leave, we are on duty. With two hundred men in the party I imagine none of us will be short of a job of some kind. I've organised two large cartons of medicines, drugs and first-aid equipment to be on hand without disturbing our main supplies. Let's hope it will be adequate.'

Jan Svensen said eagerly, 'Are you allowed to tell us the exact geographical location?'

'Yes, Jan. About sixty miles from the Russian border. The little village of Zari is our destination, in the far north of Afghanistan. The Muj Commander anticipates we should be there in three weeks!'

Conversation burst out then like an explosion—excitement, apprehension, and a general desire to get started on a once-in-a-lifetime adventure that thrilled, yet half scared them all. Everyone seemed to be talking at once, and when at last the party was breaking up, Piers Morell wandered across to Louise, who was leaning against the veranda balustrade looking out at the sheer magnitude of the mountains with Peshawar merely scattered below. It was easier to take in what they had been told when observing such grandeur.

'Louise. . .' The quiet, deep voice pulled her from her reverie. Piers Morell was at her side. 'Can we talk? If you're not too tired, that is. I know you've had a hard day at the hospital.' He smiled down at her, leaning both hands next to hers and gazing upon the same breathtaking scene.

'Of course.' A sudden tremor of anxiety hit her. After all they had been told that evening, was she now about to hear that he no longer thought her suitable? Had he already made a snap judgement that she was not the sort of female doctor he wanted after all? Maybe the people who had interviewed her had not taken into account how particular he was about such things. But that was nonsense—she cut her thoughts short, calming down to listen to what he had to say.

'I'm rather glad the others have gone off to bed— there'll be little enough chance after tonight for them to appreciate such luxuries!'

Them, he'd said, not *us*. Did this mean that he had made up his mind to leave her behind? Her heart hammered painfully against her ribs, and she could find not even the most idiotic words in reply.

'This is rather a new departure for you, I imagine, Louise, travelling abroad to such a country as this?'

'Yes. . .yes, this is the furthest I've been so far.' Her panic was receding. He simply wanted to put her at her ease.

'Your papers that I saw in Paris seemed to indicate that you did very well at your last hospital, although you were not there too long after qualifying, I believe?'

'Long enough to be confident,' she answered rather too quickly.

'Oh, indeed. I'm not doubting your capabilities for one minute. The fact that your father's a GP and runs a very successful practice in Cornwall gives you a head start. Like father, like daughter, no doubt?'

She smiled, knowing how carefully her background had been vetted. 'Anyone who admires my father—my mother too, for that matter—goes up a notch or two with me!'

He gave a nod of approval. 'Good. I'm sure you understand that this talk is necessary because, despite all the form-filling, one is never quite prepared for *seeing* the person. We bandy names of candidates about and make choices, all the while building up our own idea of the person concerned, then at the first encounter it comes as something of a surprise!'

'Surprise sounds more hopeful than shock.'

'Don't underestimate yourself, Louise.'

'I never take anything for granted, Piers,' she said firmly, his first name now falling easily from her lips.

'I'm glad.' For a second his thoughts appeared to be diverted by a silver globe of moon just skimming the peaks, then he turned his back on it, leaning easily against the balustrade. 'If I said I was agreeably surprised on seeing you, would it reassure you?'

'It helps. But I have a feeling there's something else you still want to say.'

He folded his arms against his broad chest, the aristocratic mould of his face in slight shadow. Although his eyes too were darkened, Louise was aware of his silent scrutiny, while a small frown settled between his eyebrows.

'You're right, Louise, and it's this. I'd like to know if you're thinking of getting married soon. Have you a fiancé, or. . .anything as binding as that?'

She felt her whole body tense, her fists clenched at her sides as she turned away from him, furious that such a question had touched a still open wound. She took a deep breath, then swung round slowly to face him, her voice steady. 'I fail to see that the question is relevant.'

Piers' attention was focused upon her reaction; the sudden intake of breath at his words, the tension, the obvious signs that she was trying to fight it. He sighed inwardly. And he'd thought this girl might be ideal. But, if she was so uptight, maybe she had left a lover behind, and her mind would not be entirely on the job, and that was of no use to him on such a trip. Pity, and yet. . .

He noticed the way her fair skin had suddenly flared to rose; despite her apparently cool demeanour it gave her away. 'I'm afraid I have to say the question is decidedly relevant. You see, once we leave here, we can't even be sure of mail reaching us, or any contacts being made. Then there's homesickness, the monotony of what we'll be doing, missing a loved one, all of which can't make for a good member of a team—unless of course you've been on this sort of trip before.'

Louise calmed down, his reasoning giving her a moment's respite from the bitterness of her thoughts. She tilted her head up to meet his eyes, hair taken back from her face for coolness, clear green eyes coldly magnificent as rare Colombian emeralds. When she spoke it was without a tremor, firm and devoid now of any emotion.

'The things you've mentioned hardly need spelling out, Mr Morell,' his surname stressed with heavy formality. 'Your question took me off balance for a minute. However, I accept what you say and. . .confirm that if it's your wish I'll do the job to the best of my ability. Moreover, you need have no worries on the other points raised.'

A small flicker of annoyance passed over his bronzed features. With a gesture of impatience he thrust his hands into the pockets of lightweight trousers that clung precariously to his slim, narrow hips. 'Miss Holden,' he said icily, 'I don't think I made myself quite clear. I'm asking you to say whether or not you are at present involved in a love-affair of any kind. This I have to know because such things affect people differently. Separation can so often ruin peace of mind, for instance.'

To his amazement, Louise burst into a gale of near-hysterical laughter. It stopped almost as soon as it began, her eyes unfathomable, as she said scathingly, 'Keep your job, Mr Morell! And I'll keep my private affairs to myself—perhaps that will satisfy you!' Her full breasts were heaving beneath her thin white shirt, her body shaking as she tried to control her breathing, knowing now that her chances of getting this job were nil.

Piers Morell watched this display of bravado with clinical detachment, his voice as he spoke expressing no obvious dismay at her outburst. 'Please, Miss Holden, don't be too hasty. I repeat, I am merely thinking of the good of the team when it comes to compatibility, I assure you.'

Still trembling badly and hardly knowing what she was saying, tired out and overwrought, she turned on her heel, with, 'Go to hell, Piers Morell! I'm afraid I'm not your idea of a perfect candidate after all. Just too bad!'

She flounced down the wooden steps and made her way across the lawn without a backward glance, vaguely wishing she had not slaked her thirst quite so much with whatever it was she'd had to drink. On reaching her room she was mightily relieved to see that Monique was dead to the world, and Louise did nothing more than fling off her clothes after splashing her burning face with cold water, and fell into bed with a groan of relief and was asleep in seconds.

On opening her eyes cautiously next morning, she was not surprised that her head felt like a football, and it took a little time to raise it from the pillow. At length, with a soft 'Ouch!' she heaved herself up on to one elbow to see that Monique's bed was empty, a note propped against the clock:

> From today no more hospital duties, so don't worry. See you in the dining-room for lunch, afterwards we're all going shopping, etc.   M.

Louise swayed slightly as she read the message. It no longer applied to her anyway, so she might as well take a shower and see about getting a plane back and out of this place. Once ready for the day, she sat down and tried to organise her thoughts. What sort of a fool had she been to talk to Piers Morell the way she had? She blamed it on the drink, but was convinced now that that was only part of it. A wave of severe reaction had been triggered off inside her; the shock of being jilted, to put it bluntly. This had been expected a year ago by her family at home, but had never happened. Everyone had marvelled at the stoic way she'd wrapped wedding presents and returned them, written letters and, last of all, sent back her engagement ring to Raymond's parents. Raymond at that time had taken himself off on a walking holiday in Austria with the girl of his preference. His mother and father had been devastated by the happenings, and later had told her own parents how proud they must have been of her for the way she had been bearing up.

But as a doctor herself she should have known there was no short cut to overcome shock. It gets at you in some way or other, she thought—even lies in wait when you tell yourself how clever you are that you've taken a new job abroad and completely thrown off the trauma you've gone through.

Now she had discarded what would have been one of the most satisfying experiences of her life. She stood up suddenly, pulling back her shoulders. She would make new plans. The cream dress she wore, the only one she'd brought with her knowing she would be in working gear most of the time, made her feel better. The shoes that matched were simple but expensive; the one luxury in a very limited luggage. Now that none of that really mattered, she felt cool and sophisticated, and what the hell, she would forgo breakfast and head for the nearest travel agency.

She slung her handbag over her shoulder and flung open the bedroom door.

'Good morning, Louise. I trust you slept well?'

Piers Morell stood there, tall and immaculate in bush shirt and trousers, his face unsmiling, a briefcase tucked beneath his arm.

CHAPTER TWO

FOR a brief moment Louise simply stood where she was, riveted to the spot, as she stared at Piers Morell. Then she collected herself, stepped out into the corridor, and closed the door behind her. 'Good morning,' she murmured. 'I—er—missed breakfast.'

He put his head to one side, thrusting his lower lip out slightly, and began walking with her towards the public rooms. 'I think maybe there are more important things for you and me to discuss, wouldn't you say?'

A niggle of irritation went through her. 'Don't patronise me, Mr Morell. What I have to say will take far less than a minute.'

He gave a wry smile and led her into a small writing-room, pulling up a chair for her nearest the open windows, then sat down himself. 'You'll allow me to order some coffee for us?'

Feeling somewhat ashamed of her petulance, she gave him a muttered, 'Please. . .'

They both had black coffee, and for Louise at least it seemed to have remarkably recuperative powers. She felt now that she could say what had to be said, and the whole thing would be over and done with.

Piers was opening the briefcase he had with him, but, before withdrawing anything from it, he met her eyes as she watched him. 'I have your documents and return tickets here, with all you need for travelling back to Paris. And on to Cornwall if you wish.'

He said no more, just put the case aside at his feet, then folded his long legs and sat back in the deep wing-chair, viewing her speculatively.

She was nonplussed. This was not quite what she'd expected. 'I thought that by now you would be turning the discussion into a lecture on my bad manners,' she said, with disarming candour.

He closed his eyes for a second as he shook his head. 'We're not at university, neither are you at work on the wards as an overworked, underpaid houseman!' His smile was compassionate, and briefly she caught a glimpse of him as a doctor at work, dispensing care, understanding, endeavouring to show tolerance to the entire human race.

'I'm sorry about last night—it was unforgivable of me,' she said quietly. 'All I want now is to leave and not hold up your plans for the journey any longer.'

'You've forgotten one thing.'

'Yes?'

'You haven't yet received my permission to leave here and go back to Europe.'

Louise stared at him, her lustrous eyes clashing with his stone-hard ones. 'But you said——'

He broke in to stem the flood of words he knew were about to pour from her lips. 'What I said was that I had your documents here and that you *could* return.'

'I see no point in hanging about here,' she retorted swiftly, feeling her anger rise again. 'It's quite obvious that you're enjoying this cat-and-mouse game, but I am not!'

'Believe me, Miss Holden, this is no game—it's deadly serious. Maybe I've underestimated your grasp of the situation.'

She met the icy gaze unflinchingly. 'Let me assure you, I stick to what I said last night about refusing to discuss my personal affairs. I believe I'm well qualified to do the job that was offered me, and I'd be fully prepared to take whatever comes under difficult circumstances. Other than that, my life is my own, and I do not intend my confidential relationships to become an appendix to my CV!' She stood up, holding out her hand. 'Now perhaps you'll let me have my papers and I'll take up no more of your time.'

'Sit down, Miss Holden!' his voice roared.

The command was so totally unexpected she obeyed immediately.

'Now perhaps you'll listen to me for a while. I do not like changes in my plans at the eleventh hour, and that applies to members of my team.' He leaned forward in his chair, his voice now back to normal. 'I've had time to think about your reaction last night. I believe you possess the sort of indomitable spirit and determination I need for the job in hand. This is the sort of thing that can rarely be defined at a formal interview; that's why I like to try and get to know my final applicants by other means. Therefore, although I may be sticking my neck out, I'm prepared to ask you to stay on and become a member of the team. That is, provided you're willing to consider this on my terms?' he finished curtly.

Her heart began thumping with relief as well as apprehension, but she said calmly, 'Just what are those terms, Mr Morell?'

'That your strong will be channelled into situations where it would do the most good in the job you'd be doing. The question I put to you last night was more or less answered by your reaction. I wish to know nothing more about it. As you say, it is your personal life, and therefore, always provided you keep it personal, it should not intrude upon your duty to the party as a whole.' His dark eyes softened slightly. 'I'll accept that we all have problems of one kind or another, but it's keeping them at bay that's the trouble. If you can give me your assurance that these things will in no way interfere with your colleagues, I repeat, I'll be prepared to have you join us.'

Louise's heart swung from joy to foreboding and back again, as she said quietly and firmly, 'You have my word.'

'Good,' he said briskly. 'Then you'll not be needing these just now.' He picked up the briefcase and snapped the locks shut, glancing at his wrist-watch. 'So, I think we'll get ourselves to the bazaar this morning and buy some gear that will make us look a little less. . .Westernised.' His eyes went over the trim, beautifully tailored lines of her dress that only seemed to enhance the perfection of her figure, and the implication in his next words was obvious. 'You'll change, of course. Ten minutes, OK?'

She was about to round on him for the mocking insinuation of his words, but stopped herself just in time, turning on her heel with a murmured assent he probably didn't hear as she hurried to her room. As she stepped out of the dress she was wearing, and pulled on white cotton jeans and a cool striped T-shirt in shades of blue, she could still hardly believe her good fortune that Piers Morell had decided to have her join him. It gave her the shakes when she realised just how close she'd come to wrecking her plan on principle. But she was damned if she'd budge from the things over which she felt deeply, and she would not change for anyone. Nevertheless, she had to admit that lately she had developed a habit of exploding over certain issues, yet knowing that at heart she had a reasonably equable nature. In a way, she comforted herself while collecting up shoulder-bag, sunglasses and cash, perhaps these new outbursts on her part had become something of a safety valve against a far worse catastrophe. Possible suicide was not the least of it in her darker moments.

The Khyber Bazaar was spectacularly busy despite its being a Friday, the Muslim sabbath. The main street teemed with horses as Piers Morell gave Louise a hand out of the taxi he'd summoned to take them from the hotel. They walked through a warren of narrow lanes squeezed between stone and wooden houses, some of which were so close together it would have been possible to step from the upper windows into the room opposite.

The bazaar was sectioned off into the sale of food, jewellery, spices, cloth, tin trunks and leather ammunition belts. Money-changers sat in the central square.

Piers strode along at Louise's side, somehow contriving not to lose sight of her in the bustling, jostling crowds. He changed some Pakistani rupees for a handful of Afghanis—about a hundred to the pound—and stuffed them into his pocket with a grin. 'I've arranged that we meet the others outside the cloth bazaar, when we can get fitted up,' he told Louise.

Monique, Jan and Alain were already sifting through garments that would make them feel part of the scene, the men acquiring long cotton shirts and baggy trousers, and a scarf which had many uses—handkerchief, towel or turban—and a flat woollen cap. Monique and Louise bought long-sleeved cotton shifts, tent-like and cool, as well as scarves large enough to cover everything but their eyes. Amid much giggling and chortling, not to mention haggling, the clothes were paid for, then Piers said blandly, 'We mustn't forget to buy our *pattus*.'

'What the devil's that?' Alain enquired in a diplomatic undertone.

'A light woollen blanket. Like a Scots plaid, it can have many uses,' Piers said, then asked to see the items, before they equipped themselves with five good desert-brown blankets for four pounds each. They thanked the shopkeeper and returned to the ever-moving stream of humanity where the blazing sun seemed to concentrate solely upon the bazaar. After refreshing themselves with cups of sweet green tea, they took a Vespa taxi back to the hotel, where the comparative calm after the babble and noise they'd left behind was unbelievable.

Monique and Louise spent an hour resting on their beds, both stripped down to minuscule bra and briefs, before having their evening meal at sundown. Louise flung her hands above her head and stretched with a blissful sigh.

Monique performed a more complicated version of the same thing. She glanced at Louise with a grin. 'So, what do you think of Piers Morell now that you two 'ave met?'

'I suppose you've heard what happened last night?'

'*Non*. I guessed you were about to 'ave the final interview with the boss. Nothing more.'

Louise was hesitant while she watched two flies careering around the ceiling lamp-fitting. 'Well, it didn't go off too well, I'm afraid.'

Monique raised an eyebrow, then partially sat up. '*Sacrebleu*! Do not tell me 'e 'as changed 'is mind about taking you on?' She was obviously shocked and disappointed.

'As it happened, he asked me about my love life, and I had no intention of telling him.'

Monique gave her friend a long, perceptive gaze, then burst out laughing. 'Good for you! 'E asked me the same, but at least I was only too 'appy to tell 'im I was once again free with no complications!'

Louise grinned. 'It sounds as though you were far more polite than I! Anyhow, this morning he seemed to have reconsidered, and offered me the job.'

'Thank 'eaven! But that follows. I think 'e would rather have opposition than submission. If 'e believes it to be justified.'

'Whatever he thinks, Monique, I imagine it's set me off on the wrong foot with him.'

'*Absurdité!* We are all entitled to our opinions.'

Louise pushed back her hair from her forehead with a loud sigh. 'I think he's a tough nut, and once he forms his own ideas about someone, he's not quick to change.'

Monique sat up suddenly. 'Look, Louise, I don't want to pry into your private affairs either, but knowing what we 'ave in front of us, it would be far better if you forget trying to work out what Piers Morell is all about and think of yourself. By which I mean there is obviously a good reason why you wanted this job—that probably goes for the entire team. So just relax and conserve your energy—you're going to need it!'

That evening, over fresh lime drinks, they all sat on the veranda talking about final plans for their departure the following night. Jan seemed restive suddenly, and stood up to lean against the palings, looking at Piers. 'I've been thinking about the situation out here, Piers. If I'm right, hostilities have never officially been declared between Afghanistan and the Soviet Union, which makes it impossible to apply the Geneva Convention?'

Piers nodded, his white, open-necked shirt dazzling in the mellow coolness of the night. 'Right. In the same way, strictly speaking, neither is the Red Cross able to operate its usual role. That's why it's so necessary for us to get through in semi-secrecy in order to do as much as we can for both sides if necessary.'

'Yes, I see the point now.'

Alain finished his drink and stood up. 'Well, I say roll on tomorrow night. The sooner we get started the sooner we can give that much-needed help.'

One by one they drifted off to bed. Louise was about to leave when she realised she was once again alone in Piers' presence. 'Another drink, Louise?' he offered.

She smiled. 'I don't think so, thanks.'

'You're not worried about the journey ahead?'

'Quite the contrary. In some ways the thought of it is even more satisfying than what we do for patients at home.'

He got to his feet, his large frame briefly blotting out the full moon from her sight. 'Well, there will never be enough of us to do everything that's crying out for attention. We can only do our——' He broke off as a man hurried from the hotel out to the veranda.

'Dr Morell, it is the telephone, would you come, please?'

'Excuse me, Louise.' He left with the man immediately. 'Sleep well!'

She had barely returned to her room when the bedside phone rang. It was Piers. 'Louise, sorry about this, but would you mind coming over to the hospital with me? There's the equivalent of a red alert over there. Warn Monique that she'll most likely be wanted once we see exactly what the situation is. Come down as soon as you're ready—I'll be in Reception.'

At the hospital things were chaotic. One of the resident doctors tried to explain amid the noise in the casualty section. 'It happens always when we least expect it,' he said, smiling philosophically. 'Spasmodic fighting breaks out constantly along the border between rebels and Government troops, and tonight there has been a particularly bad skirmish, it seems, with more casualties of a severe nature than usual.'

Piers nodded. 'Right. My assistant here and I will cope with the major casualties if you can get the victims sorted into some sort of urgency. Meanwhile, I've arranged for my colleagues to come over as soon as they can.'

Piers looked worried as the man went off. 'We'll help, of course, but I'm not having our party working right up until just before we leave tomorrow evening. It's almost midnight now. We'll all do a couple of hours or so each. I'll go and have a word with Alain.'

When he came back from the telephone, Piers and Louise helped with the thankless task of selecting the major from the minor injured. Stretcher cases surrounded them on the floor and flowed outside and beyond the entrance, with mostly gunshot wounds, some by accident, some design. Two hours ago a sixty-year-old man had been watering his roses in his courtyard when an anti-personnel rocket had hit the mountain above, showering splinters and causing serious injuries to him and other members of his family. Two members of the theatre nursing staff brought in the injured man, but his wounds were such that even before Piers started to operate on him he died while the anaesthetic was being administered.

In the makeshift operating theatre, victim followed victim. Louise worked as Piers' assistant. Her own experience in this field was limited, but she managed on his instructions.

'This young boy will never hold a gun again,' Piers murmured, as a boy of no more than eighteen was brought in and work started on the amputation of the right hand and three fingers on the left. Time was of no importance.

'Which sutures?' Louise asked at length, her head beginning to throb with a dull ache through sleeplessness.

Piers didn't raise his eyes from his task. 'No sutures in the case of the arm, in order that the soft tissue will not contract and leave the bare bone. . .'

She was aware of his voice coming and going in her ears, and for one awful moment she thought she was going to faint, but the coloured mist cleared from her eyes as she heard Piers saying, 'Delayed sutures may be inserted after a few days to bring the skin edges together, so long as there's no infection.'

Eventually, having remained on duty far longer than Piers had intended, they left the theatre, Alain and the others having appeared to take over. In the small room used temporarily as an ante-theatre, Louise was washing at the hand-basin when Piers said flatly, 'The man of sixty was as good as killed while watering his roses, one of the staff said. I agree with her. There he was amid the apple and cherry trees, his family around him, going about his pleasant tasks, then. . .boom, out of the blue. . .' He moved to the basin, washing and drying his hands and arms vigorously, face drawn with exhaustion, voice disgusted. 'I ask you, what sort of world are we living in?'

Louise discarded her theatre garb, unable to answer, yet agreeing wholeheartedly. She wouldn't have moved but for the fact that she felt Piers touch her arm and lead her outside to the cool, sweet night air. The night was so deceptively peaceful.

She barely remembered stepping into the taxi that had been ordered, and they were back in the hotel within minutes, it seemed. She felt marginally improved as

Piers said at her elbow, 'I have some brandy in my room. On the way I'll get the night porter to put a sandwich or two together for us, and we'll have it on the veranda.'

She waited there, unable to demur. The sights and sounds of the last few hours had been far too awful to allow her to sleep. She didn't think she was hungry either, but if Piers wanted to go in search of something it was up to him. She sat down in a basket chair, staring absently.

Piers returned with a laden tray, poured brandy and soda and passed one to her with a tired smile. 'Here's to us.'

'And others like us,' she murmured, sipping the burning liquid, and feeling it seize her throat. Life was returning to her limbs. 'Quite a night!'

He sat, long legs straddled before him, eyes unfathomable, face unsmiling. 'This was the last thing I wanted to happen to us all, but it was impossible to refuse. Also, I didn't want to advertise the fact that we were leaving tomorrow—today now, would you believe?' Across the lawns was the faintest glow of dawn light behind the mountains, pink and gold. 'Have you done much theatre work?' He rubbed his forehead impatiently. 'I just forget.'

'Nearly a year.'

'You were good.'

'Thanks. If I'm not speaking out of turn, so were you!'

Piers gave a smile, one that softened and lifted the entire contours of his face to one of sweetness. 'A compliment is always welcome, Louise. What we did tonight was under de luxe conditions in comparison with what we'll no doubt find at the mountain clinic, but at least it's given us an idea of what we're in for.'

Louise took another longer gulp of brandy, fancying a sandwich as she handed the plate to Piers, then taking one herself. 'You've been on these sorts of trips here before?'

'Yes, but one never really gets used to them. There's always a feeling of outright anger followed by intense frustration.'

'It must be worse when you leave, too.'

'Right. The fact that there's still so much left to do is like leaving a sinking ship.'

'I can understand.'

His eyes hadn't left her face. 'I could tell that tonight.'

'This journey ahead of us—is it. . .very difficult?' she asked, wanting to ward off any hint that she might be casting for further approval.

Piers did not answer at once, only studied the remaining liquid in the bottom of his glass, then tossed it back before saying, 'Difficult, yes, but quickly forgotten once there.' He stretched his body, flexing his muscles, then stifled a yawn. 'I get the impression that there have been other "difficult" things you've had to deal with in life?'

Perhaps he thought the drink would loosen her tongue, but he was mistaken. Louise stared across the gardens. 'We all do at some time or other, and I'm no exception.'

He hauled himself to his feet suddenly, looking down at her. 'I know that. Nevertheless, don't let it. . .harden you.'

She gave a hollow laugh. 'After what we've seen tonight, that's rich!'

'True. It hasn't made you want to change your mind about accepting the job now?'

'No, of course not.' While he was speaking, Louise felt her perception must have been heightened by the brandy. Quite suddenly a wave of submerged anger hit her. Piers Morell must have known she would agree to his offer to stay. He'd planned the whole thing and she'd danced to his tune! Her blood boiled. His arrogance was beyond the pale! Of course she was right. Hadn't he told the others that he and Louise would meet them at the bazaar the previous morning? He'd had no doubt at all that she'd be with him!

'Something wrong, Louise? You look as if you've just lost a pound and found fivepence!'

'In principle, I think I have.'

He grinned. 'Oh, dear, I'm implicated somewhere!'

'I don't like being manipulated by you, that's all.'

A sudden perfumed breeze stirred the dusty trees, lifting soft tendrils of hair about her face and cooling the texture of her skin. Piers looked at her quizzically. 'Manipulated? Surely not?' he said lazily. 'But do carry on. I might as well hear all these grievances before we set off.'

There was amused mockery in his tone, but Louise didn't care as she plunged in. 'Well, despite the heavy moralising you did yesterday about your prospective staff—in this case, myself—possibly unnerving the rest of the team with my tales of woe, you'd made up your mind that I'd fall in with your plan to go with you anyway. That is a fact, isn't it?'

He moved from the balustrade where he'd been standing and leaned his hands on the table, his taut face inches away from hers. 'Yes,' he replied in a clipped voice. 'Is that such a bad thing? Was it too much to expect? Let me tell you it was a question of *hoping* that you'd go along with me, relying upon your own assiduousness, and I planned accordingly. Come on, Louise, snap out of it! You've worked marvellously tonight and I'm well satisfied. There, does that put the record straight?'

She grinned, wondering what really lay behind those dark, intelligent eyes. 'OK, Pax!' Sleep was sweeping over her in gigantic waves, making her incapable of thinking or saying anything else.

Piers knew this and pulled her to her feet. 'It's time you got to bed. I'll leave word that you're not to be disturbed. I've arranged for refreshments for the others. I'm sure Monique will be just as dead beat when she gets back to your room.'

'OK. . .' she mumbled. She would have liked to have

said more to him about something that had annoyed her;
but at this precise moment she just could not recall what
it was. . .something about manipulating. . . She heard
her name as they walked into the hotel. It was Piers at
her side.

'Just one thing: I am not setting up a vendetta against
you. Please remember I have to consider the welfare of
three other people as well as yourself. Now, just sleep
soundly and forget everything.'

In her room, Louise tried to think clearly. Her addled
brain made it impossible, but one thing of which she was
certain filtered through. Piers Morell made her feel like
a recalcitrant child one minute, an adult bitch the next.
Heaven help them once they were on the trip! And,
despite her desperate fatigue, she knew it was up to her
to calm down, to look at things more broadly. Just
because Raymond had treated her so appallingly it didn't
mean the rest of the male population was standing by to
do the same. She had to stop analysing Piers Morell's
motives and wipe the slate clean of her conclusions about
him clean. The sooner the two of them got on to the
same wavelength, the better. And that particular wavelength was doing the job they had come out to Afghanistan to do.

That afternoon each member of the party awoke after
some eight hours' sleep and recovered from the night
before in their own particular way. Piers was seated on
the veranda with a pile of papers, checking lists in case
he'd overlooked any minute detail, including such sun-
dries as flea powder, shoelaces and packets of dried soup.
Alain played nine holes of golf at the Peshawar golf club
in the torrid heat with Jan; Monique and Louise went
for a swim.

From then on followed a flurry of discussion and final
planning, and, by the time dinner was over and they'd
rested once more for an hour or two, it was an awesome
thought that it could well be several more months before

any of them lay or slept on a comfortable bed with a mattress again.

Louise was unable to sleep. She closed her eyes, still thinking of the patients she'd helped Piers with. It seemed almost cruel to withdraw their assistance from the beleaguered little hospital. But there was the small group of medics working at Zari who eagerly awaited their arrival so that they too could re-acquaint themselves with the things everyone took so easily for granted.

To a background of Monique's gentle snoring, for the hundredth time Louise wondered just how long it would be before tempers flared again between Piers and herself. She'd vowed to keep things cool between them. Yet, under the hard conditions that faced them, it might not always be she who took the lash of his tongue and cold iciness of his scorn.

As if to highlight those fears, as they gathered later in restrained excitement outside the hotel for a midnight departure, Louise could already hear Piers' voice raised in anger on the phone just inside Reception. Their transport, due to take them to a secret Mujahedin destination, had not yet arrived, and this did not bode well for the good start they had hoped to make.

CHAPTER THREE

IT WAS a full hour later when the Land Rover for which they'd been waiting, camouflaged as an ambulance and driven by a smiling Mujahedin, put in an appearance. Bags and luggage were stored, the main supplies having gone on ahead to the rendezvous where the real journey on mule and horseback was to start. At last they were ready to leave. Piers made sure the rest of them were reasonably comfortable in the back.

'Any problems here?' he queried, seeing two tough-looking Mujaheddin in baggy trousers and two Muslim ladies smiling cheekily back at him from behind their veils.

'We're fine!' came the collective answer.

'Let 'em roll, then!' Jan Svensen called, as Piers slapped the side of the vehicle and sprang up into the front passenger seat next to the driver, and they were off. In fact they shot away like a bullet from a gun, from then on racing and bumping across the green April countryside, hurtling through police checkpoints and villages, scattering everyone and everything in sight. In front, the driver, Nazim, was beaming with satisfaction at their progress, and at one point picked up another rebel who was squashed unceremoniously in front with them. Madly they careered on through the night, Nazim still smiling as they crashed into pot-holes and Piers' head bounced painfully against the roof. Then after three hours of extreme discomfort they stopped at a small town and climbed stiffly out.

Monique shivered, wrapping her arms around her against the chill of the early morning. 'Where the 'ell are we?'

No one had time to answer before they appeared to be

surrounded in a narrow street by a collection of wild-looking, bearded men carrying rifles. The party was told to return to the Land Rover, and the driver took them through an iron gate set in a high mud wall. There was nervous tension in the air, and the vehicle was rushed through as quickly as possible.

Inside, young Afghans were everywhere. Alain murmured, as they jolted to a stop, 'I imagine these must be the Mujahedin we're travelling with.'

Piers, in the company of Nazim, took them to a house at the end of the courtyard where they were shown inside to rest. There were dirty blankets on the floor and tea was provided. One hour later they moved off again with just one more important checkpoint to clear before arriving at a mud village perched on the edge of a ravine. It was here they were to begin the real part of their journey.

Under cover of darkness the long caravan of horses, rebels, supply mules and donkeys travelled at night where possible to avoid any remaining daytime patrols. Risking morning and evening hours too, the Mujahedin were careful to stick to the mountain shadows as much as they could, disguising the animals with earth-coloured blankets in case of trouble.

All roads that had been under Soviet control were not yet freed, and necessitated their still picking their way across country via the old silk and sheep trails that wound through the high passes of the Hindu Kush. Piers told them airily, 'Not for nothing was the tail-end of the Himalayas known as "The Killer of Hindus."' Which the flagging medical team considered one of his more outlandish understatements, and not very funny.

That particular morning, it was three o'clock, and eight days after leaving Peshawar far behind. A half-moon had risen like a shy young girl, neck bells on their few panniered donkeys tinkled musically, and the shouts of the drovers provided a bass accompaniment. Dogs barked in the distance and a solitary cock crowed.

Astride her horse, which she had named Kismet, Louise blessed the gradually gathering morning light across the sky. It meant not only food, but rest and sleep, giving a few blissful hours of oblivion from the heat, and the hunger pangs that struck regularly. They were by no means starving, but the complete change of diet to near-primitive food, and in quantity just above subsistence level, was more an influence on a state of mind than body. Yet she was surprisingly fit. Monique admitted to feeling the same, even though her French culinary sensibilities must have been sorely tried.

As had become their practice, the party rode together as often as they could. Now they were climbing steadily towards one of the soaring passes, Monique slightly ahead with Alain and Jan, Louise flanked by two young soldiers, who, like the rest when safe, had quickly overcome their shyness at talking to two unveiled women. And, despite Louise's lack of the language, once it became a question of survival communication between them all was rapid by some means or another. The leader of the men, Commander Anjum, a quietly polite academic man with a good grasp of English, as had his two aides, soon saw to it that barriers began to fall.

Piers was riding at the head of the convoy that morning, negotiating with the Commander for the following day and the one after that. Supplies had to be constantly checked, food offered along the way and all the other needs of a group of people on the move met. Now, as dawn began to leave them more exposed, a sense of silent urgency gripped them as the protection of night moved away. If there was a clear sky a Russian plane might pass over. It could be a reconnaissance, but it might not. Peace had apparently broken out, but old habits died hard and the men were constantly on the alert.

Piers reined in at Louise's side, his face taut as it often

was at this time of day. 'We must get a move on, Louise,' he told her briskly. 'Anjum's had word through his informers that there could be some kind of "reception" waiting for his men, and that includes us. We have to cross this pass and get down into the valley before resting.'

She glanced across at him. 'That's the good news, now what about the bad?' she quipped, wondering what some of Piers' rich patients would say if they could see their suave consultant now, resplendent in colourful Afghan clothes, features sunburnt, eyes alight with purpose.

He actually grinned, which hadn't happened for days. 'Let's think—how about sleeping beneath a roof instead of a rock today?'

'I'd definitely classify that as five-star!' she said, and laughed back at him, not realising how the morning radiance illuminated her face, the emerald depths of those eyes capable of making a man's heart beat faster in these wildly primitive surroundings.

Piers rode back thoughtfully to the head of the column. He still found it difficult to understand Louise Holden. She had not complained, and was shaping up well under these conditions, but he had the feeling it was a penance she was inflicting upon herself, and sooner or later she would have to pay for it. He hoped not. Certainly not while they were on the trip, anyhow. Selfish, he knew, but he still had qualms about taking her on.

The trip was far from over yet, he thought irritably; female company was not a luxury he allowed himself on such occasions. Nevertheless, there was a damnable stubbornness about Louise Holden that both intrigued yet exasperated him. She certainly had a temper, that was for sure. It would take a man of iron to tame it. He switched off his thoughts abruptly as they approached a dangerous area. He swung his mount round and rode back to Louise, reaching over and grasping the lead rein on her horse. 'We're almost at the top of the pass, and the descent is likely to be very slippery and dangerous. Go easy now!' His voice rang out with an impatient note of command, dark eyes anxiously raking the sky and the deep valley below.

Louise said nothing; she was just grateful for what little help she could get. The only riding she'd done since possessing a pony as a child had been a two-week riding holiday at a rodeo ranch where her sister was happily married to the owner. Now it was all a question of making friends with Kismet and hoping for the best. The impatience in Piers Morell's voice no longer bothered her as it had at first when it had seemed as if he'd been venting all his annoyance on her. That was nonsense, and she'd tried to put Monique's advice into practise and look after her own well-being. Nevertheless, the trip wore down the nerves, fraught as it was with the ever-present uncertainties and danger that lurked around each corner. The distant whine of a plane, although perhaps harmless, still had them diving for cover beneath outcrops of rock, or their blankets. There was the sudden clatter of helicopters too, maybe only on a legitimate flight, but the sight of them, whether at dawn or dusk, could be equally menacing.

Tempers frayed in the heat, small irritations took on gigantic proportions when sore feet, aching backs or throbbing heads had to be endured. Piers was responsible for their team, and so far he had shown nothing more than an admirable composure with no sign of temperament. If he was right—that even now they were in imminent danger of being scattered by trouble—then he was being remarkably cool. . .

Kismet was by now already starting to pick her way daintily down the terrifying descent. Louise's heart was in her mouth. She was petrified, parched, and could hardly breathe. This was when she preferred the darkness, the time when she could be as scared witless as she really felt.

She riveted her eyes on the rhythmic, slowly heaving

rump of the horse in front of her. Piers rode the creature with great aplomb, tugging at his reins with one hand, half turning in the saddle, while with the other hand grasping her lead rein. He turned suddenly, glancing back at her, while she prayed he wouldn't let go the rein which to her was as vital as an umbilical cord between them. He said easily, 'It may be better to dismount if you're not too happy; it is rather steep here.'

She gulped nervously as her horse slithered a few feet, trying to get a foothold on the damp shale and sending a small shower beneath her. 'I'm fine, thanks, I'll stay on Kismet as long as she's OK!' she called brightly.

'Up to you!' Piers called over his shoulder tersely. 'Don't say I didn't warn you!'

Ahead, she could see Monique and Jan gingerly descending on their mounts. She tried to concentrate on Monique so that she needn't look down at the mind-boggling gradient. What was her friend thinking at this moment? A city girl, born and bred in Paris, she'd confided to Louise that she hardly knew one end of a horse from the other. But she was game enough to keep it quiet.

Piers was calling her for some reason. Briefly she lost her concentration. Kismet stumbled and almost went down on her knees, but managed to regain her footing, though not before Louise had lost her own balance, causing her to be pitched into thin air, certain she was about to disappear clean over the Hindu Kush and out of sight. She must have screamed blue murder.

There was a loud shout and two firm hands caught her, while another pair helped her straighten up. One of the soldiers had seen it happen a split second before Piers could reach her. She was still gasping like a dying fish and shaking like an idiot. The rebel soldier, giving a broad grin of white teeth, touched her companionably on the shoulder, then left her with Piers.

Both his strong arms were holding her steady, twined about her, and she clung to him. His body was all that

stood between her and eternity, and it was firm, strong
and smelt of sunlight and cold fresh air. 'Are you OK,
Louise?' he asked anxiously.

'I. . . I can't move,' she screamed faintly, averting her
eyes as she caught a glimpse of Monique and Jan ahead,
looking like pin-men.

She swayed as Piers waved the rest of the column on,
then he tightened her to him again. 'There's no need to
panic, Louise. I thought you had no fear of heights?
Take a few deep breaths, and don't look anywhere else
but at me.'

She did as he'd said. For a moment her trembling
seemed to subside; the morning breeze tugged at her
hair, sending it about her face. She loosened an arm
from his grasp to push it back, then concentrated on
lifting her eyes to his. The sudden flapping of the wings
of a giant eagle sent her clutching him frantically.
'I. . .can't, Piers. . . I can't do it! I'll never do
it. . .never!' she ended on a loud miserable wail. 'Leave
me here, please. . .and you go on!' she gasped, sobbing
with sheer terror.

Kismet was nuzzling her waist, as Piers snapped
sharply. 'Don't be a fool, Louise! We've got to get going.
This is no time for female hysterics!'

Trembling again, wildly, outrageously, and hating
herself for her weakness, she cried out, 'I know! But I
can't move. . . I can't!'

'Right! I'm sorry to have to do this, Louise, but
dangerous situations call for dangerous measures!' He
raised his hand swiftly and gave her a brisk slap on the
side of her face, bring a wave of rose colour at the
contact. . .and with it a howl of derision from her.

'You swine!' she yelled, touching her face with one
hand, still latched on to him with the other. 'How dare
you? You downright despicable. . .!'

His handsome face registered the same swift and
devastating power as the golden eagle now wheeling
above waiting to swoop on its prey. He jerked her even

closer to him, disregarding her struggles and thrusting
his cool, hard lips down upon hers, raising them briefly
to growl, 'Stop making a fuss, woman, do!' Louise
resisted even more at the blatant cheek of his
remark. . .but his lips were kissing her in such a way
that the fight was leaving her, the crazy sensation of
soaring high above the world with an eagle was too
real. . .

She struggled to resist him again despite her precarious
position, but with the urgency of his mouth on hers she
whirled deeper and deeper now into a pool of rainbow
colours, wanting to sing for joy, before soaring high
again. Common sense prevailed and she pulled away,
only to find him laughing at her. Strong white teeth
gleamed between the beard and moustache he'd grown
of necessity. Thoroughly enjoying the joke, he threw
back his head in great good humour.

'You see, what did I say?' He laughed jubilantly.
'Treatment for maximum effect needs to be short, sharp
and concentrated!'

She pounded his chest with balled fists. 'You low cur,
you. . .you exhibitionist!' she shouted, saying the first
thing that came into her head, knowing she dared not let
go her hold on him. 'You importunate, scurrilous,
contemptible——'

Piers stemmed the flow with another kiss, then said
infuriatingly, 'Well, you seem to have recovered. I think
we'll set off again now!'

His 'treatment' must have done some good, because
when he loosened her from him she made a grab for
Kismet. She even attempted to mount her despite her
still trembling limbs brought on by shock, but now
superseded by the impact of Piers Morell's effect on
her—although she would admit it to no one. That in
itself made her livid at the thought of that arrogant,
conceited, supercilious fiend!

Piers was restraining her from mounting the horse,
handing her the reins. 'Sorry, this is where I insist you

walk,' he instructed brusquely. 'You'll be OK—just hang on to Kismet now, she'll get you down.'

Speechlessly Louise did as she was told, conscious of her faintheartedness, and Piers' moment of domination over her. The thought was so mortifying she felt unable to think clearly of anything other than his haughty presence, as she murmured through parched lips, 'Don't worry about me,' which gave her a crumb of dignity. 'I don't need it.'

'We've almost covered the worst,' he told her. 'From now on it's a good stride down. It'll give her a break too, poor little devil,' he muttered, patting Kismet's flanks. He tucked the creature's lead rein back over her neck, then left Louise, to urge his own horse down the mountainside and meet up with some of the others.

She gave a rueful grimace as she watched Piers go. Just like a man—for a moment there she had actually imagined he had been concerned for *her*! Which was crazy, when she wanted nothing from him whatsoever. He'd given her the chance to take part in this trip, had helped her over a squeamish moment of her own, and that was it. No doubt she'd be able to repay that debt in some way before the end of their stay in this country. How, she couldn't think, but sooner or later she would even up the score.

She was conscious of the remnants of the column trailing behind her as gingerly she moved on, her limbs now beginning to act like her own. Already it was getting extremely hot, daylight revealing the mountain peaks in their full glory, which could mean danger.

The company of men, animals and supplies were an incredibly easy target, straggling as they were down the snake-like paths. The plodding mules carrying the medical supplies were constantly being pushed, slapped and yelled at by the muleteers. As the sun rose higher and the land evened out, Louise's attention was fastened on the irrigation channels they had now reached, clear cold water gurgling deliciously in the heat, maize shoots creating a green carpet, walnut trees and mulberries casting deep pools of shade in an otherwise——

A warning shout alerted them. It seemed to slice through the ragged procession like fork lightning. Planes, at their first sighting high in the bright sky above them, zoomed over the mountain tops. Piers tugged Louise down to the ground with a near-rugby tackle, flinging a *pattu* over them both. There was an uninterrupted whine, and far, far away a dull explosion seemed to vibrate through the earth. Piers did not move, although he threw the stifling blanket off their heads. Louise looked up at him enquiringly. 'The danger's over—it's all right,' she said primly, trying to escape the arm that tethered her.

'Keep still,' he ordered, all but smothering her with the blanket. 'Sometimes they have a nasty habit of returning. . .'

Her heart beat fast with nervousness. She kept her face buried deep in her arms, at the same time trying to flatten her body against the hard ground.

But the planes did not come back, and gradually the tension lessened and normality took over; with it the peaceful silence of their surroundings. Slowly, warily, Louise got to her feet, dusting herself down, Piers doing the same, and they waited for the rest of the team to regroup. Jan Svensen was still looking decidedly European despite the elaborate turban he wore on his head; the trouble was that no one had yet had the time to tell him how to tie it!

'Hi!' he called. 'Still all in one piece, I see. Near thing—makes you hungry too!'

The house in which they were to stay that day was in a village of mud-brick buildings surrounded by high walls. On arrival, Commander Anjum, who was of medium height, thick-set and wearing khaki combat jacket and trousers, black army boots, chequered scarf and a flat woollen Chitrali cap, was surrounded by his men and already established in the large yard. A meal was in preparation using an earthenware oven sunk into the ground, the bottom full of a glowing red wood fire. The baker was squatting on his heels attending to the thin, flat oval-shaped bread they knew as *nan*, his assistant extracting it once cooked, and handing it round with hot, sweet tea.

Later, while Alain and Jan were in animated conversation with the Commander, Louise and Monique had the chance to slip away for a wash of sorts from a pitcher of water which they shared. They were directed to natural facilities on the edge of a dried-up river-bed, and for more serious operations this meant crossing the same river-bed to the cover of bushes opposite.

Following a meal of stringy goat meat and rice, the party, by now spent and exhausted, took to their sleeping-bags. The girls were given the luxury of their own room with mud walls and a high window.

Monique was rubbing her buttocks with great care as she eyed the floor. '*Mon Dieu*, I do not think I shall ever sit on a 'ard chair again, let alone sleep down there!' she groaned, throwing off her dress and scrambling into her bag anyway. She sighed wearily as she settled at last. 'Fingers crossed no one is in need of medical treatment! I see someone 'as already left our first-aid bag in the corner there.'

Louise stretched out in her bag next to Monique. 'They'll have to shake me back from the dead if I'm needed,' she murmured. 'I must say I never expected us to turn into a mobile hospital on the hoof, so to speak! Surprising, though, the number of minor things we've dealt with already. Some of those men had the most terrible foot blisters, but they never complain.'

Monique gave a little squeak. 'Please, do not mention blisters! I just cannot get used to my boots when we 'ave to walk—it is torture!'

'I know,' Louise agreed, tucking her hands behind her head, then over her eyes as brilliant sunlight bounced off the whitewashed walls. 'Do you think we'll ever reach

Zari? I mean, I feel as if I've been on this trip since I was born. Is there any other kind of life?'

But her words fell on deaf ears. Monique had already fallen sound asleep, and Louise took only seconds to do the same.

In just another second, it seemed, someone was shaking her by the shoulder. With a groan she heaved her body over to push the irritation away. Then from a distance she heard her name. . .'Louise, wake up, please!'

She rolled on to her back, eyes flying wide, cheeks flushed with sleep. Piers Morell was looking down at her, as he said sympathetically, 'Sorry about this, but there's a woman in the village who needs our help.'

Still dazed, fair hair tumbling about her shoulders, Louise sat up, mumbling, 'Right—OK. Just give me a moment to splash my face.' Fortunately they had saved a little of the water from the night before, and its icy coldness pulled her together. She threw on the Muslim dress and a thick Afghan cloak over that, tying a scarf at the back of her head and sweeping her hair back with it as she ran out to where Piers waited at the door with his medical bag.

'I don't quite know what this is going to involve,' he explained as they followed a veiled woman, 'but if it happens to be a birth, some of these women are not too keen on male doctors; that's why I wanted you with me.'

When they came to the village centre they went inside a small house on the perimeter where animals stood tethered in the lower storey. From an upper floor, the plaintive sound of wailing female voices met them. The rebel soldier who had accompanied them to act as interpreter, lest Piers Morell could not convince them he was a doctor, grinned widely. 'Very good! Maybe a baby soon, hey?'

Piers nodded. 'Perhaps. We will help if we are given permission to enter the house together.'

The man went off and was back in minutes. 'Come!'

It was a mean room, which appeared to be full of black-robed women rocking back and forth, wailing in a toneless dirge despite their arrival. The noise was relentless but no doubt intended to assist on just such occasions. 'Quite definitely a birth,' Piers murmured as they stood hesitantly on the threshold, while the soldier urged them forward before leaving.

A young girl lay on a thin mattress on the floor. She was no more than fourteen years old, her long black hair damp with perspiration, her brown eyes dazed and huge with fear and pain. Still wearing voluminous, dusty black clothes, she screamed in terror as the singing became louder.

One woman, evidently her mother, who had been praying volubly while at the same time giving instructions to the girl above the general clamour, looked up and flung her hands out to Louise in a desperate plea more eloquent than words. Louise, trying to put aside any thoughts on hygiene, gave the young girl a quick, reassuring smile, opened the medical bag for a pair of latex gloves and prepared to make a quick examination.

The baby seemed to be in immediate danger of asphyxiation from the cord which had been compressed between the foetal head and maternal pelvis. Swiftly Louise moved aside for Piers to give his diagnosis, which he did, very quickly. Meanwhile, even in this life-and-death situation, the mother of the girl had darted forward to cover any sighting of her daughter by a man other than her husband. But such rules had to be waived.

'We must work fast,' Piers stated. 'She's in the second stage of labour, as you see. Normally I think it would mean a Caesarean immediately. If we don't do something soon they'll both die anyway. There are some forceps in the bag—I could give it a try,' he said dubiously.

'Let's chance it,' Louise muttered. 'The poor kid hasn't many.'

'Right. I agree.'

By a swift combination of signs, and relaying instructions from Piers via the soldier outside and back again to the chanting women, hot water was soon made available. Piers, meanwhile was murmuring soft encouragement to the girl in her own language, and giving her an injection that quietened her for a while. She was by now practically unconscious after heaven knew how many hours of futile pain, and after chewing on a plant supposedly meant to induce a hypnotic state that had been given her earlier by the assorted relatives clustered around the bed.

While Piers collected up the few pieces of equipment he needed, Louise managed to persuade the audience to move back from the girl's bed. Finally, with the help of the soldier, they agreed to huddle in a corner, anxiety and fear mixed with suspicion in their tear-filled eyes.

'She's lost a great deal of blood, which we can't spare to replace, even if we had it on hand. She's bound to be suffering iron deficiency anaemia at the very least,' Piers muttered as they contemplated the imminent fight for life amid the awful conditions. He cursed under his breath. 'OK, here we go! Let's try the forceps. Thank God the cervix is fully dilated. . .'

By now both he and Louise were kneeling on the floor, Piers making the first attempt to reach the baby. The girl's cries were no longer audible, her strength was failing rapidly. Time was not on her side. After the third effort, pausing only for Louise to wipe perspiration from Piers' brow, a firm grasp was established on the foetal head with the instrument. Piers managed to draw it gently forward just enough for Louise to free the cord from the child's neck, then gently swab the eyes and nose with gauze. When the final contraction came, presentation was completed with shoulders and body.

'Cheers,' Piers murmured. 'We have another little male rebel!'

A ripple of soft voices had gone round the room, a dozen pairs of dark eyes fixed on Piers' quick smile of satisfaction. He wiped his forehead again with the back of his arm, smiling at Louise as she cut and tied off the umbilical cord. Afterwards Piers held the child up, giving a light flick on the soles of its tiny feet and thereby raising a feeble cry, bringing a louder gasp of approval from the watching women. He handed the baby to Louise, and tenderly she wrapped the sturdy little brown body in a clean piece of cloth and placed him in his mother's arms. The young mother had managed a drowsy smile; her eyes, although still glazed, were now beautiful as she took her son to her breast.

Piers and Louise did what was necessary thereafter to take care of mother and child as best they could. Later they passed the new offspring to its grandmother, and Piers, with complete confidence fully restored between them, told her in her own language to be sure that her daughter continued to bathe her body with the antiseptic lotion they would leave her. Fortunately, he told her, it had been their good luck that her daughter had needed no stitches. They handed over iron tablets and orange juice for the young mother, as well as milk powder for her son, and that was as much as they could do.

It was, it seemed, more than enough, especially as the new child was male. Hot water in abundance was given them to clean up, the samovar was charged and tea served. Eventually, amid songs, music, tears and laughter, they left the rejoicing family. Mother and baby were sleeping at last; the survival of both was now far more than just a slender possibility.

Outside, the morning was still young. Louise pulled the scarf from her hair, allowing a soft, dancing breeze to lift it from her neck. Piers walked at her side deep in thought, the rebel soldier ahead of them, his job done also. The sky was of the palest blue, the towering mountains russet-gold, bare and stark, but the most amazing thing of all was the light, so pure and shining as to be crystalline. It enhanced everything, every bush, every stone, every flower.

Louise raised her face to the blueness above, inhaling

the newly scented air and saying quietly, 'A pity we shall never know how the mother and baby get on.'

Piers, whose mind was still dwelling on the awful inadequacies of the peasant family they had just left, and, even worse, the nagging guilt of a job poorly done, said abstractedly, 'That young girl *should* have had a Caesarean section with all the attendant safety measures.' His brow was creased in frustration. 'Yet she's only one of millions more in a similar situation. . .God!' He punched a fist into his palm. 'Why on earth does it have to be this way?'

The eruption of words caused Louise to glance at him quickly. She knew exactly how he felt. 'We did what we could, Piers—you particularly. It was a marvellous job, given the conditions. Both mother and child alive too. The problem is massive, but no one person can take it upon themselves to feel entirely responsible.'

He stopped beneath some mulberry trees, as if hearing her for the first time since they had left the family behind. 'Maybe, but. . .' He raised his shoulders dejectedly, unable to say more, leaning against a tree trunk, setting the medical bag down and staring out across the wide, sunlit panorama of mountains, valleys and sky.

Louise too remained silent, as both drew comfort and solace from the natural beauty in front of them. The formidable eternity; the never-ending cycle of love, hate, birth and death. . . She was lost in thought, her long, dirt- and blood-stained Muslim dress fluttering against her slim legs, her hair flecked with gold as on sunlit water, her profile reflective as she spoke. 'Being in such a country as this makes me feel that we in the West are no longer truly in touch with the real world. This is where it is, here amid the harshness of reality and poverty. We're so civilised, and bowled over when faced with such things.' She turned to him with a smile. 'But it ever was, as my father would say!'

Piers gave a laugh, the tiredness leaving him suddenly. 'Well, I suppose we mustn't take ourselves too seriously;

but, regarding our deficiencies as members of the human race, we can only keep on trying!'

'There's one other thing I must tell you.'

'Yes?'

'This morning was the first time I'd helped at a real birth. Theory, yes; practice, no. Just standing in during my training. That was the real thing and, quite honestly, I was petrified!' She gave a tired grin. 'No doubt I shall wish I hadn't told you that when I'm in my right mind!'

'You are in your right mind, and it was a good job you did, and,' his eyes twinkled, 'don't think I'm in the habit of giving out verbal bouquets!' He picked up her cloak and his bag. 'Come on, you need all the sleep you can get now—we move off at dusk.'

They reached the mud-walled house and its area beyond. Men sat around talking, attending to their animals, or rolled in blankets on the ground fast asleep. Louise took the cloak from Piers, murmuring her thanks and going to her quarters. As she stepped into her primitive room her mind suddenly felt freed of all worldly things. Exhaustion, utter and complete exhaustion, she told herself as she stretched on the floor again alongside Monique, who appeared not to have moved by so much as a hair of her head. For a moment she willed her thoughts to resist the sleep of oblivion. There was something on her mind after all. It was Piers Morell. She had never met anyone quite like him. One minute he had the fearsomeness of the eagle they had seen; the next, he was as gentle as a dove. Never in her wildest dreams would she understand him. Yet there remained one area where her belief in him this far was unshaken.

She might detest his arrogance, cynicism and conceit—particularly when administering his 'cure' for her attack of nerves, which she could hardly recall now for embarrassment—but she considered herself fortunate to be working with such a man. According to Monique in one of her more serious moments, Piers was one of the world's leading surgeons, who used money from the rich to care for the poor, particularly in the Third World. Whatever else this man was, more so once they reached Zari and returned to some semblance of orderly life, her respect for him had grown.

CHAPTER FOUR

THE journey unravelled for another week, each day much the same as the one before. Louise had not been called upon again to perform any further midwifery; instead blistered feet, wrenched ankles, insect bites and varied minor stomach upsets seemed all that was necessary to test their skills.

Louise and Monique had very little contact with the men of the team in the ensuing days. Piers, Alain and Jan rode out with the Commander to where ambushes might be expected, and which meant their route had to be re-worked. Night riding was still preferable, but now and then morning and evening hours had to be used. On one occasion, when an unidentified aircraft was sighted at dusk, Commander Anjum lined up all the animals nose to tail along a river-bank until the potential danger had passed. This slowed the party down still further but was a necessary precaution.

The following evening Piers talked to the assembled medical team a few hours before setting off on the night's trek. They were sitting on the ground around him, studying an open map. 'We have to cross this area here,' he explained, as they drew in close to look. 'It's a place called the Plain of Zermat. I'm not saying it will be easy, but the Commander insists this should be the route we choose. It may take a little longer, but he must drive hard, and those are his orders. We have to obey them.' He grinned suddenly with sympathy, his dark eyes looking around at their earnest faces. 'I hope your feet are still in good condition—there's more walking to do rather than riding, I'm afraid!'

As they already knew, Piers tended to be a master of understatement. The plain they were to cross end to end was some twenty-six miles, covering a hard, unpleasant surface of stony ground over which they stumbled constantly and tripped in the dark. Then came a belt of loess, topsoil dust as fine as powder and about six inches deep. It was like walking in cotton wool, and although the night was perfectly still, clouds of choking dust rose and hung on the air. Impossible to escape, it got into everything: ears, nostrils, mouth, hair and eyes, shrouding them all with a pale grey coating which aged them overnight!

The crossing did in fact take eighteen hours, with the final instruction Piers slipped in, 'No talking!'

'I am too scared to anyway,' Monique whispered in Louise's ear, as at one point they had only one mile between themselves and the Russian border, giving them a glimpse of soldiers moving in front of the lights.

Once they had crossed the plain and made the final agonising steps back to the safety of the mountains, Monique and Louise almost gave up; they were in shreds. Jan and Alain found them both squatting on the ground too fatigued to move another inch. The men tried inducements, encouragement, everything they could think of, until at last Jan said brightly, 'I've got it! Just hang on to your horse's tail and he'll drag you over the boulders!'

'But they're as big as sofas!' Louise wailed.

''Ouses!' Monique joined in, in desperation.

Alain helped them both to their feet. 'Come on now, girls—you can do it!'

Jan was grinning at the look on their faces. 'Sure you can!'

And, with neither of them wanting to let the female side down, they did. Even the rebels were whatever the Afghan word was for knackered, and, throughout, it created a great feeling of comradeship between them all. They pressed on, small incidents standing out in Louise's mind—like the man they came across selling snow! Nearing the end of the journey a few problems dogged them. Louise overcame a bout of dysentery; Monique suffered bronchial pains. Jan, Piers and Alain kept their ailments a mystery, depending on how low-spirited they happened to be at the time.

Strangely, it was the rebels who kept their morale high, particularly when one would come to the daily 'clinic', as delighted as a child that a nasty gash they'd attended to several days before had quite healed. The men's touching praise was all the thanks they needed.

At last came the memorable day when Piers announced that the end of their journey was at hand. 'We're heading for a "safe" house,' he told them with a grin, the thick dark beard enhancing the lean jaw, brightly intelligent eyes and even white teeth. 'We happen to know that a party's being prepared for us, and you all deserve every moment of it!'

It was quite an occasion, of the sort Louise never thought she would experience. About two hundred of them joined in the revelry; although the food and drink was much the same as usual, the dancing, singing and exchange of family gossip, and endless talk about the trek, complimenting each other on taking just twenty-three days for the five-hundred-mile journey, made them drunk on sheer elation alone. They learned also that Commander Anjum and his band of men would be lodged not far from Zari for the time being, and firm friendships were cast, some forever.

Next morning the team could hardly wait for their first view of Zari on entering the village. When they did, they stood gaping. It had to be a time-warp; the scene was straight out of Biblical times.

Piers, on horseback, alongside Louise and Monique, shook his head slowly. Jan and Alain did much the same. The 'hospital' they had been longing to see was exactly three large mud-walled rooms.

No one moved as they took in the green clearing, the mud-walled building protected from the sun by a few overhanging trees. Nearby, they saw the lightning flash of a small waterfall busily tumbling into a wide, clear stream gushing over flat brown stones. . . Alain murmured, 'Are we dreaming?' and seemed to speak for them all.

But within seconds incredulity gave way to delighted amazement, for their arrival had been the signal for a mixed company of people to burst like an explosion from every direction, laughing and shouting a welcome, local children, men and women happily all talking at once as Piers and the team dismounted. Immediately they were enveloped by hugs, kisses and greetings in English, French, German and Australian. A tall, thin, ascetic-looking man stepped forward, gripping Piers by the shoulder. 'You are Piers Morell!' He smiled warmly. 'I am Colbert—Dr André Colbert. Welcome! How we've waited for this moment! It is so good to see you!'

Monique and Louise were helped from their mounts. 'You must wash and rest. We will look after you, and then we will talk!' two smiling women assured them.

In a daze, Louise looked anxiously towards the band of Mujaheddin tending their animals. 'They will look after themselves, do not worry,' someone said, as they were led unprotesting to where cool, clean, sparkling water was poured into large bowls for them, with even a small canvas screen for privacy. Afterwards, the food, though plain, was a veritable feast. The host team did everything they could that evening to entertain them royally. Despite the fact that they were leaving themselves in two days' time to make the same hazardous journey back to Peshawar, nothing was too much trouble for them.

The following day, after a plump, warm-hearted nurse-midwife had shown them over the men's quarters, then the women's, they all sat outside in a small patch of cultivated garden which had been nurtured by successive teams who had come to Zari.

Alain was sitting smiling benignly at the woman. 'I imagine you cannot wait to get back to England?'

'Quite the contrary.' She laughed ruefully. 'I don't know how I shall bear tearing myself away from here. I've loved the place, despite the conditions. It's surprising what you can become used to. The people here are so grateful for all we do.'

Monique sat hugging her knees. 'I cannot believe you look after so many patients, it does not seem possible.'

Dr Colbert joined in with a laugh. 'They are mostly keeping away today because they know there is a switch-over! A pity, really; we just get used to each other, and then a fresh team has to come in. Still, it's to be different this time—it's to be handed over to them, isn't it?'

Piers smiled. 'Fortunately we're entering happier times, we hope. We'll try and keep in touch with you, though, and we won't let Zari founder if we can help it!'

They spent the rest of the day listening to how the clinic was run, and going over the layout. The outgoing staff were zealous in their praise of the local medical workers, and the way the villagers tried to help.

The following evening at dusk, Dr Colbert and his subdued little team were ready to leave. Piers had already handed over mail due to them from Peshawar, and letters were exchanged to be posted home via Peshawar. As the caravan assembled, and addresses, messages and small gifts given and received, there were few dry eyes as the long train of animals, medics, and a fresh contingent of Mujaheddin embarked on the hard road back to the border.

Piers and Louise stood watching the endless trail gradually disappear into the gathering darkness. 'They seemed a good crowd,' he said thoughtfully. 'Let's hope we can continue the same way.'

'We will,' Louise stated firmly. 'We have to. There's more at stake, really, handing over to a staff that may be without a qualified doctor for goodness knows how long after we've gone.'

Piers ran a hand over his hair. 'There's certainly plenty to do; nevertheless, I want everyone to take it easy for the first week. We've all had a hard time and we need to get fit before we hurl ourselves into a new regime here.'

As he spoke, Louise noticed how tired and drawn he looked about the eyes. She had not heard him complain once, but subconsciously a pang of fear went through her at the thought of anything happening to him. He was the one they immediately went to with their queries and problems. Who could possibly take his place? Alain or herself? She put the thought aside hurriedly as she walked back with Piers to the area beneath the trees where most of their meals were taken.

The dwelling set away from the clinic by a few hundred yards, which Louise and Monique came to regard as their own, was a two-storey structure. The lower floor, one large room covered by a Persian rug, on which stood a low table and which was scattered around with cushions, was considered as the general common-room when things had to be discussed away from the heat. The upper floor—with an open-air lavatory on the flat roof—gave the two girls a small area each comprising a mattress, a rough mat, and a small table hand-carved by a previous occupant. Louise considered herself lucky that her mat was Afghan and brightly embroidered, and she immediately displayed it as a wall-hanging, consid-ering it to be too good for use underfoot.

'You are artistic, Louise,' Monique said. 'I would not 'ave thought of doing that.'

'We must go to the bazaar in the village and see what else there is.'

Monique was stripping off in her section of the room. 'I think we shall be too busy,' she said, and laughed shortly.

Louise thought she detected a note of lassitude in the girl's voice. Her bronchial trouble had taken its toll, and had obviously left her depressed. 'Cheer up, Monique; in a few weeks when we've regained our strength we'll be doing all kinds of things!'

Monique was splashing loudly behind a screen. 'You are right, of course,' she called. 'But Louise,' she added, reappearing, her schoolgirl figure clad only in bikini pants and bra as she towelled her face dry. 'Now that we are 'ere, 'ow do you think we shall get on with the men? Piers is so. . .withdrawn. Alain is rather too eager to please. Jan thinks 'e is—er—'ow do you say, the cat's pyjamas!'

Louise laughed as she looked up from brushing her hair out before washing it. 'I know what you mean. It may be a little difficult. We'll just have to try and understand each other.'

Monique nodded. 'I know this is true, but men are men,' she said dolefully.

Louise hung her long tresses over the bowl of water. 'Perhaps you're like me sometimes, Monique, and feel that men can be—well, quite a let-down.'

'*Oui!*' Monique snapped unexpectedly. 'It could be better if we were all female 'ere!'

During the following week, Piers repeated his dictum that none of them should work too hard, but concentrate mainly upon drawing up plans to establish a duty routine which could merge with the local staff already at the clinic. On a warm evening, Piers, clad in cotton trousers with nothing to cover his bronze torso, sat talking things over with them while waiting for the village woman to bring their evening meal. Everyone seemed in improved health. Alain and Jan were in high spirits and sprawled bare-topped beneath an apricot tree. The girls sat cross-legged, wearing one of several more Muslim gowns they'd inherited, and in which they felt more comfortable than anything else, as they relaxed and listened.

'It seems to me,' Piers was saying, tapping the end of his Biro against his lips, 'that Monique, Louise and I can handle most of the antenatal and postnatal clinics. Jan and Alain, you can give me a hand with in-patients at nights, and Monique, with a couple of the local girls, during the day. Then there's surgical work, of course—

that's where Jan and Alain come in. Louise can assist there too. In other words, it's obvious we have to turn our hands to things with which we're not too familiar, but we must help each other. I want maximum communication between us all. Is that understood?'

They talked on long after finishing their meal until a huge white moon sailed over the mountains and still the air was warm and sultry at this, the best time of day. They established certain rules used in normal hospital routine as far as was possible, and when they all went off to bed it was with easy minds.

Louise did not feel like sleep. Her brain was teeming with what they had discussed, and she did not go to her room but wandered away slightly from the hospital to where the darkness was pearl-grey and the night scents of trees and grasses gave out generously of their fragrance. The village overlooked a fertile valley; she could clearly see trees, pathways, small white buildings with large gaps in between, all etched in silver with almost English orderliness. Only the busy gushing of the waterfall invaded the silence; no alien planes in the sky, no snuffling of horses or mules as when they'd been on the long trek. She looked up. The star-filled sky was just asking to be touched, almost anything seemed possible on such a night. . .

'Beautiful, isn't it?'

It was Piers. Obviously he'd had the same idea as herself. 'Rather too good to miss,' Louise said, and smiled. He no longer looked tired but at his usual peak of fitness, and she felt a great sense of relief. Tonight he looked very much the consultant surgeon, beard shaved away completely, dark hair brushed back, in a dazzling white shirt and beige cotton trousers.

Together they strolled along the bank of the stream, his face in shadow. 'How do you think you'll cope here now?' he asked suddenly.

'It's a challenge, one that I welcome.'

'I had an idea you'd say that.' He turned to look at her

as they walked. 'Does life have to offer challenges in order for it to be enjoyed?' he asked quietly.

'It does for me,' Louise said curtly, suddenly on the defensive that he might want to know things about her which she was not prepared to tell. They talked in general for a while until she said, 'I think I'll get back now. I'm sure you value some time alone.'

She didn't wait for his reply. As she returned to her room she began to feel the old antagonism stealing over her—that he was still angling to find out about her private life, which she had no intention of revealing.

The following evening, after a fairly easy day trying to accommodate each other with regard to duties, Louise found herself on call that evening with Piers until midnight. It had been a quiet spell, and, apart from checking on the few children who were on the ward for observation, there'd been little urgency. One of the young local nurses, named Shani, shy but a good worker, had made coffee for them and set it on the small wooden balcony used mostly as an outside office and general place for medical personnel only.

Piers picked up his cup thoughtfully, drank, then said, 'I asked you last night how you thought you'd cope here. Your answer, I suppose, was satisfactory enough. . .' His eyes met hers quizzically. 'But what about Monique?'

'She feels the same, I'm quite sure,' Louise said firmly. 'Even so, I don't think she's as fully recovered from the journey as she should be yet.'

'We all had strict medicals before we came out here. If Monique had any bronchial weakness, the X-rays would have shown it,' he said dismissively. 'Isn't that so?'

'Not necessarily,' she retorted. 'A minor weakness could have been there undetected, but aggravated by that Zermat march.'

'You're right, of course. I'm glad to hear you say that. It proves that your powers of medical observation haven't been dulled!' said Piers in a lazy, sarcastic drawl which niggled her.

'Should they have been?'

'It could happen on such a trip as ours. The mental processes often slow down when physical energies are tested to the limit.'

She finished her coffee. 'If you're giving me a lecture, Piers, I'm not particularly in the mood for it.' Her pale blue Muslim dress, flimsy though it was, felt heavy about her limbs, the unmoving air was so sultry.

'What are you in the mood for? A film, a meal somewhere?' he asked flippantly.

'Nothing so civilised, thanks.'

'Civilisation is the curse of mankind in many respects. In Paris alone, there are women who don't deserve one quarter of what so-called civilisation has given them.'

Louise gave him a quick sideways glance. 'It sounds as if you know some exactly like that!'

'I do. It's trips like this that give me the chance to escape such people. My parents are the best people I know. I was born in Peking—my father was a banker out there. He and my mother have retired to Scotland now, happy just to have time for each other. They're my idea of real people.'

'You studied in Peking?'

'No, I was sent back to England for schooling and medical training. Each time I returned to Asia it was the one place I felt really at home. Nevertheless, my work's gained momentum, for which I'm glad. I earn the money so that I can return here to help these people. Bringing a team out, as I have on several occasions now, is an exercise in self-discipline and an expansion of a basic truth—survival. That to me is what life's all about.' He glanced at his watch. 'Wow! How time flies—it's midnight! Sorry if I've talked too much about myself. Maybe it's because I've just had my thirty-sixth birthday!'

'When was it?'

'The night we arrived here.'

Louise grinned. 'I couldn't have kept that to myself.'

'At twenty-six you don't need to!'

They walked back towards the compound, where the men's quarters were separated from the women's by a group of flowering trees. Out of the blue, Louise suddenly had a flash reminder of the time Piers had kissed her, still making her squirm. . .

'Piers,' she said coolly, 'you mentioned your grasping acquaintances in Paris. Was any one of them special to *you*?' Her ripple of laughter was facetious, and by the reaction on his face it seemed she'd scored a point or two.

'No, Louise! Goodnight!' he snapped, and strode off.

She chuckled. It was great to discover that she could actually get under Piers Morell's skin. She'd have to try it again!

Next day the long queue of women—more than a hundred each day, they'd been told to expect—from the village and many more miles around, snaked beneath the trees and into the small lean-to where the antenatal clinic was held. It contained a rough floor covering, an examining-table, cushions, earhenware bowl and a covered pitcher of water. No running hot water, no electricity, no X-rays; the list was endless.

As Louise squatted on her cushion that morning she arranged a large tray of bottles and jars which contained the various treatments she was able to prescribe. If short of many things, they were certainly not short of enthusiasm and maximum effort to care for the endless stream of pregnant women now waiting to be seen.

Piers entered and glanced at the notes of women to be examined. This too was a slow and tedious business, since he had to regain their confidence now that Dr Colbert had gone. Louise had already been handing out vitamins and orange juice to some of the women who had been allowed in first to reduce numbers for quickness. Yet, by some mysterious process, the queue seemed as long as ever.

Piers was wearing one of his long cotton shirts over baggy Afghan trousers which the men wore most of the time for coolness, but in which he still managed to look more impressive than anyone else. Noticing Alain's departing back clothed in the same apparel, as he left the clinic after borrowing a sphygmomanometer, Louise thought there was just no comparison. She glanced at the box file beside her, stuffed full of meagre notes on patients, and added another one, giving a small sigh with the intensity of the heat as she watched the dark, voluminous robes of a patient disappear from view. She was glad of a slight respite before calling the next mother in.

Piers had been watching her, his silence somewhat unnerving after her rather cut-and-thrust exchange with him the night before. Now he sounded somewhat impatient. 'Louise, as we neither of us know exactly what's expected of us at the moment, I suggest we work together as each patient comes in and take it from there. I think it's hopeless trying to establish any kind of selection process in advance once all the vitamins have been distributed.'

'It might be best,' she said pleasantly, having already determined that whenever they worked together she would try her hardest not to jeopardise the relationship they were endeavouring to forge, and which so far had worked well. Private and personal irritations simply had to be put to one side.

A noise interrupted her thoughts. An older woman and a very young one seemed to be engaging in a wrestling match, the young girl eventually dissolving into tears and capitulating. Piers addressed them rapidly in their own language. Both females then turned on him at once, screeching and screaming, showering him with words, incoherent but furious, until he shouted a loud command to them both. Whatever it was, the order was immediately effective.

'What's the trouble?' Louise asked anxiously.

Piers made a grimace. 'The young bride of thirteen can't understand why she's been brought here by her mother. Apparently she's been practically dragged from their home in the village. Pregnant, no doubt. That's the first thing to establish, anyway.'

The morning's work had begun in earnest. The young bride was indeed pregnant. Piers completed the examination after quietening the mother, and a form was then filled in with basic details. The girl left in awed silence, the mother's arm firmly clamped around her while she volubly chattered and gesticulated, a broad smile of satisfaction on her face.

By the end of the five-hour stint, the rest of the queue had to be turned away and told to return in two days' time, Piers having decided that each clinic should have a limited quota of hours during the week in order to give the team time to look after the in-patients on the 'wards'.

After a short break that afternoon, Louise was making her way back to the hospital from the staff quarters. She was thinking about food: thick, juicy steaks, curry, ice-cream. . . They were as yet not properly organised. The last medical team had apparently told the village woman and her helpers what sort of food to prepare, but they had all been so busy no one had thought about getting down to the changes they wanted. She met Monique just coming off duty for her break.

''Ello, Louise.' She smiled. 'Oh, I am so 'ungry, but I 'ave a leetle surprise for everyone tonight!'

Louise felt her taste-buds leap to life. 'Don't tell me you're going to cook for us, Monique?'

'Per'aps; who knows?' Monique seemed more animated suddenly. 'But I think everyone will be 'appy!'

Still smiling, Louise made her way into the clean, whitewashed building, thinking that Monique was looking better, so perhaps at last she was recovering.

In one ward the few male patients lay on mattresses on the floor. Behind a partition were the females, and a section with a degree of privacy was in the second. The

third, a smaller section, was for the children, combined
with a small medical supplies store. Three young women
from the village had been taught the rudiments of
nursing by consecutive medical teams, and were kept
under the sharp eye of a mature Afghanistan woman who
had been trained up to sister status at a general hospital
over the Russian border. When she returned to Zari, the
village in which she had been born, it was on the
understanding that she would not leave. Her name was
Sabia, she was married, tall, aloof and beautiful, but as
yet had little to say to the team. Now she was watching
the two auxiliaries busily taking temperatures, pulses
and carefully recording them. A big advantage was that
most of the staff could understand enough English to
make communication less complicated; that too had been
picked up from former medical teams.

As Louise entered, one of the young girls called her
and rushed forward, and, despite being told not to do
this by her friend Shani, another auxiliary, seemed
unable to restrain herself in her agitation. She tugged
Louise towards a young man lying on his bed with his
face contorted with pain. 'He has. . .' the girl indicated
her stomach, making a grimace across her attractive,
dusky-skinned face.

'Yes, I will come. One moment.' Louise collected the
ward report book kept on a shelf, and looked up bed
number six, which was an easier process at that stage
than trying to get her tongue around some of the names.
The man had been admitted two days before with severe
abdominal pain, since when he had smiled each time
they went near him, insisting 'pain gone'. Now it looked
very much as if it had returned, and Alain's first
suspicion of appendicitis could have been correct.

Alain appeared at her side, hearing the man's groans.
'When this man was first brought in, Sabia thought he
had a piece of shrapnel in his side. Yet it did not seem
so from my initial examination, but without X-rays. . .'

He shrugged disconsolately. 'We'll have to get the poor devil seen to, but what do we do for an operating theatre?'

Louise looked at him sharply. 'The same as the others have all this time, Alain—make do!'

He seemed not to have heard her and suddenly turned on his heel, muttering that he had to speak to Piers. Five minutes later Piers came in, a puzzled look on his face. 'Anything wrong with Alain?' he demanded.

She felt uncomfortable. 'I. . . I'm not sure. I. . .know he was complaining of a headache earlier. . .' She hoped the excuse would suffice. Despite her own irritation at Alain's wishy-washy attitude about the non-existent operating theatre, she hated the thought of being disloyal.

Piers cursed under his breath, saying briskly, 'I'd better examine this patient—he's obviously in a bad way.' He confirmed that it was appendicitis. 'We'll operate within the hour. Give him a premed now—Omnopon, and Antropin to help dry the secretions.'

So far they had not been required to perform real surgery, but their pre-plan was that wherever possible two nurses would always assist Alain, Piers or Louise. 'Who shall I call on duty?' asked Louise.

'Let's see. . .Monique and Jan are in their rest period. Get Monique, would you, Louise—she can make up the time later.'

Louise thought of Monique's earlier depression, and, despite the girl's happier mood that morning, being suddenly called to an op under less than primitive conditions could be extremely harrowing. 'Would you mind if I ask Jan?' she said quickly. 'Monique's still not a hundred per cent.'

A look of impatience crossed Piers' face, as he agreed. 'OK, but remember, we just can't afford to mollycoddle anyone here!'

A small area at the end of the men's section had been partitioned off for more serious treatment, and with a long, flat wooden table and little else this was where the patient was transferred for the appendicectomy. Jan and Louise set out the mobile equipment they required, instruments, dressings, drugs, everything sterile in aluminium-covered canisters. They themselves wore green disposable theatre-wear in the unsatisfactory environment. Hot water had been prepared by the bucketful, and at Piers' instruction the patient was given an intravenous injection to obtain swift unconsciousness, with a small amount of diazepam added for an equally quick return to ultimate consciousness for an operation of short duration.

Jan was stationed at the patient's head, supporting his chin as he lay flat. Louise was in charge of instruments, swabs and sutures, and in that primitive theatre Piers performed their first general surgery at Zari. The young rebel was beginning to stir just as the final suture was tied off. Piers' relief was obvious by the quick grin he gave them as he raised his head. 'Phew! Fifteen minutes—not bad!'

'Too right,' Jan murmured. 'No need to give him another shot, and with luck there'll be no vomiting.'

Two soldiers at convalescent stage took the place of hospital porters and carried their colleague back on a stretcher, by which time the man was fully conscious and smiling happily.

CHAPTER FIVE

THAT evening the team sat beneath the trees in the warm dusk sharing their meal with the local staff, including two male orderlies and anyone else who happened to be on duty at that time. Word had travelled fast. Already villagers were offering help as well as small amounts of money and food, anything to keep their hospital going.

The meal that evening had been adequate, but Louise felt almost disappointed after her conversation with Monique about something special! Not to be taken seriously, she knew, but it was unlike Monique to say one thing and mean another.

Once the staff had left to return to the wards, conversation between the team became rather stilted, and it was soon apparent that there was a certain tension between Alain and Piers. Jan seemed perhaps unaware of it as he sat back contentedly plucking away at his guitar, the notes falling softly and rhythmically on the pungent night air.

Piers, who had been giving a great deal of concentration to cutting an apple, suddenly looked up at Alain, saying tersely, 'Now that we're on our own, Alain, I think you should explain exactly what happened this afternoon to prevent you from seeing to the appendectomy patient. You gave me a rather hurried explanation which I had no time at that point to analyse, knowing that a patient needed attention. Please don't misunderstand me. I've no intention of harbouring animosity between us, but, as I insisted when we first came out here, anyone nursing a grievance must bring it out into the open. It's the only possible way we can solve it. Now perhaps you would go ahead and give us your version.'

Louise felt uneasy, quite certain that Piers was giving

Alain the iron-fist-in-the-velvet-glove treatment. Alain's round, genial face looked unguarded suddenly, as if all the kindly, outward show of warm-hearted beneficence had deserted him. It was a fleeting impression Louise had, but she was not surprised to see what looked like a moment of panic change into a slow, self-deprecating smile, as he said goodnaturedly,

'I know, Piers, just what you're thinking. It was my fault entirely, and I offer my apologies here and now. I must say too that your idea that we all talk things through remains an excellent one. . .'

Jan stopped strumming, his journalistic mind no doubt impatient with Alain's cumbersome response. 'Get on with it, then, Alain. We can hardly wait!'

There was a ripple of amusement between them all, as Alain too retained his smile and carried on.

'You see, Piers, without beating about the bush, I suddenly lost my nerve when actually confronted with the need to do the op. Don't ask me why it should happen. I have performed hundreds of such operations in my time, but quite unexpectedly the thought of working in these primitive surroundings—well, I just couldn't face it. Therefore I could not put this man's life at risk, feeling as I did. That was why I came to tell you about it. Maybe I phrased it badly. I might have said something about a headache, I do not remember, but to be honest, I was mightily relieved when you took over.' He looked round at them all as they sat over the discarded remnants of the meal, his earnest face and quiet words gaining silent and understandable sympathy from them all. 'I can assure you, of course, it will not happen again. I hope it never happens to any of you. It is not a good feeling, I assure you.'

As he finished speaking, they were still silent, only too well aware that it could have been any one of them; but Monique was looking abashed, as if her countryman's momentary lack of confidence was a black mark for France. 'Alain, we understand.' She shrugged, appealing to the ring of faces for mute approval. 'We all 'ave these leetle—er—'appenings. I tell you, the best thing is to forget it.' She gazed hard at Alain with her large, expressive eyes, and he seemed comforted by them as he mopped perspiration from his brow with a large white handkerchief.

Piers gave a tepid smile as if it pained him to agree with Monique. 'How right you are, *mon amie*! I was just hoping everyone would feel that way!'

Louise nodded. 'Quite definitely—I'm surprised nothing of the sort has cropped up earlier. That overland journey took more out of us than we realised.'

Jan grinned widely, returning to his guitar strings. 'If that is the worst that occurs during our stay here then we are lucky indeed!'

The words had barely left his mouth when the all too familiar buzz of planes overhead intruded as it had not done since the team had been on the move. 'Down!' Piers yelled, as with one concerted leap they flattened themselves into the ground, arms over heads, hearts racing, ears pounding as the machines seemed to fly in low above them. . .then to their intense relief flew on and away.

'Reconnaissance!' Piers declared, looking up into the sky. 'That means they've heard of our presence. Anjum told me it might happen. From now on we should be more careful when we sit out like this. Quite likely they'll come back.'

Monique was smiling. 'Do not worry! I will cheer you all up. I 'ave a treat for us. Come to the common-room and I will show you!'

Once they were gathered there, Monique fetched her suitcase, and, acting like a magician, flung the lid up with great panache and withdrew a handful of coffee-bags and a large packet of chocolate to be shared between them.

A great cheer broke from them.

'Monique, *chérie!*' Louise said happily. 'You couldn't have waited for a more perfect psychological moment!'

'You're wonderful, Monique!' Jan laughed, hugging her.

Just one cup of coffee each and four cubes of Cadburys put them all back to a peak of excitement they'd not reached since their arrival party. Even Alain and Piers seemed to overcome their coolness towards each other. Piers was breathing in the coffee as the steam tantalised his nostrils. 'Umm! Monique, how on earth did you manage to keep such a treat for so long?'

The French girl giggled delightedly. 'I do not know—it is fortunate it 'as not melted! But I 'ave imagined this moment many times, and luck was with me!'

Monique's generous action had completely wiped out the smouldering tension that had been brewing among them. Now all the old comradeship was back again, and the rest of the evening was spent singing songs to Jan's music, retelling travellers' tales, and finishing up listening to the BBC World Service News on Piers' treasured short-wave radio before they all dispersed for bed.

In their room that evening, the two girls chatted more happily than they had for days, and Louise was surprised when Monique said suddenly, 'Piers is a very clever man.'

'Diplomatic too,' Louise added, sitting up in bed applying lotion to some irritating insect bites on her legs that refused to go away.

'Ah, that is it!' said Monique. 'I agreed with 'im about Alain. Poor Alain is an honourable Frenchman, he should 'ave told us 'ow 'e felt, without waiting until Piers announced it so that Alain 'ad no choice but to make 'imself look. . .weak.'

'Poor guy,' Louise said, putting the lotion aside, 'we mustn't blame him. Thank heaven Piers saw it as a problem we're all likely to face. It just so happened poor old Alain had to be the first. I don't think this will happen again!'

Monique yawned. 'I certainly 'ope not! Otherwise we are going to be in for difficult times!'

Those words were to be prophetic three weeks later. It had been brought to Piers' notice that their food supplies were becoming uncomfortably low. At breakfast, with only Jan and Louise with whom to discuss it, they went over ways and means, but arrived each time at the same conclusion. Two of them would have to drive into the village and endeavour to buy the basics they needed. If there was nothing, they would go on to the next village, and the next, and so on.

Jan looked worried. 'I suggest that you leave Alain and Monique and me to hold the fort, Piers, while you and Louise see what you can do.'

Piers nodded. 'If I can have a word with Commander Anjum, we might just be lucky, otherwise it looks like yet another course on how to slim in six easy lessons!'

Later that evening while they were drinking tea, after eating the bowl of rice that was dinner, Piers explained to the staff, 'You see, while the war was on there was a scorched-earth policy. Now it's rather too soon yet since the Soviet withdrawal for the villages to have planted enough crops for immediate use. In Kabul, for instance, there's a coupon system provided for supplies of fuel, food and commodities such as soap and cooking-oil. This is good, but it doesn't apply to these isolated areas where the people have suffered just as much if not more.'

Alain looked concerned. 'There's hardly time for us to grow much here ourselves. Besides, the soil must be just about the stoniest in the world.'

At length it was agreed that Louise and Piers would set off with the Afghanis Piers had bought in the money market at Peshawar. 'If money's no use, we may have to resort to selling our drugs,' he said, 'and that's the very last thing I intend doing.'

That night, Louise was exhausted as usual, and fell asleep as soon as her head touched the pillow. . . But long afterwards, it seemed, she heard organ music. The strains of the 'Wedding March' rose up about her ears, and she was running wildly from the church. Raymond, his arms around another girl, was laughing and jeering as her wedding dress disappeared from her body. . . They were taunting, their faces grotesquely huge as they came nearer and nearer to her. . .

'No! No! Get away. . . I hate you. . . I hate you!'

Her own screams wakened her—she was bathed in perspiration, but her ragged breathing calmed down as she realised where she was. . . Slowly Louise sat up, dropping her face into her hands when with untold relief she looked up to see the Afghan rug on the wall. Trembling, she tried to regain the calm she had found lately, one that had convinced her the nightmares had gone forever. She looked across at Monique's bed, and in her bemused state was surprised to see it empty.

'*Chérie*! Not again!' Monique's voice was shaking slightly as she walked back into the room. 'Is there anything I can do? Some water, per'aps?'

'Please, Monique. I'm sorry to disturb you this way. . .' Louise took the water, giving her a quizzical frown in the cold half-light before dawn. 'I've just realised you were already up. Is anything wrong?'

Monique pushed her fringe back from her forehead, her face quite white in the shadows. 'It is nothing. Maybe the rice upset me, I do not know,' she said dismissively. 'But I worry about you, Louise. I am not sure you tell me the truth the first time you 'ad a bad dream?'

Louise gave a wan smile. 'You're quite right, Monique, I didn't. Perhaps it's time now that I did.'

Monique scrambled back to her bed, lying down as if exhausted. 'There is no need, Louise. But,' she paused slightly, 'if it will make you feel better and stop those awful dreams, then it would be better to do so.'

Louise sat with her back propped up against the wall, gazing at the brilliant embroidery, muted now in the grey light. 'A year ago I was jilted at the church on my wedding morning,' she explained. 'It was the worst moment of my whole life—the shock, the humiliation. I feel I shall never get over it. . .'

'Do you still love 'im?' Monique asked quietly.

'Oh, no. I'm quite convinced of that. He. . .he swept me off my feet. I, who am supposed to be the level-headed one of the family! It all happened so quickly. . .' Louise gave her friend an outline of how Raymond's attractions had completely overwhelmed her, how it had nearly wrecked her studies. 'I must have been mad,' she said softly. 'The only thing left now is my shattered pride.'

Monique nodded. 'I think it is that which bothers your subconscious more than anything, Louise. You are very sensitive to such things, despite your so-English cool, calm attitude.'

Louise smiled. 'You're right. I think you would have dealt with it very differently.'

'*Mais oui*! I would have said all those things that you stored in your mind instead of 'urling them at him. Now you suffer with these nightmares because of it.'

'Have you ever been madly in love, Monique?'

There was a short silence while Monique stared at her hands, then she said slowly, 'All I can say, *chérie*, is that I 'ave been. 'E lives in Paris and 'as just gone back to 'is wife. Not long ago 'e talked of divorce and marrying me. I believed 'im for a time, but then I say it is finished. *Mon Dieu*, 'ow I loved that man! I think it is over and I try to forget.'

They talked on for a while, gradually falling silent, then eventually to sleep. By morning there was no time to refer back to the conversation. Fresh anxieties of a more practical nature were already nagging at Louise, as she sat down to a meagre breakfast before preparing to leave for the village with Piers.

Jan, Alain and Monique gathered round the battered old Land Rover, which was a highly prized possession of the clinic and used whenever petrol was available. With the Mujahedin camping in and around the village this was usually a possibility, but not quite so straightforward as filling up at the pumps.

Piers grinned as he tested with the dipstick. 'Full, Allah be praised! Dr Colbert told me that by strange and mysterious means we would more often than not find the tank full, and the vehicle ready for use!'

'Yeah, that's true!' Jan said, reporter's notebook tucked beneath his arm. 'One of the guys told me that once a Russian vehicle's captured, the petrol it contains is worth almost more than the transport itself to the Muj. So this is our lucky day!'

Louise climbed in beside Piers. 'We can use it!' She beamed at the others. 'Back soon!'

Alain stood aside as Piers turned the engine over. '*Au revoir! Bonne chance* with the food. We'll have steak *aux frites* for preference!'

'I'll see what we can do!' Piers grinned as they lurched across the rough ground. He waved to the others, looking as happily carefree as a man newly released from captivity. 'Wow, it's good to be driving again!' he said, handling the vehicle with skill. 'Civilisation has its uses,' he confessed with a smile, knowing that Louise recalled his earlier condemnation of it—her own, too, for that matter.

'Let's hope we manage to get something for the cupboard, otherwise life's going to be rather more primitive than usual.'

'That's for sure!' Piers sang out. 'Still, I'm hoping to see the Commander. He'll help if he can.'

'Great character!' Louise said ten minutes later, allowing herself to look down at the deep, rocky ravines, the hairpin bends, then up to the solid phalanx of snow-capped peaks, ridge after ridge to the far horizon.

Piers glanced across at her. 'Hope we're not bucking too much in this thing—we seem to run out of road every now and again.'

Louise was clinging on to the hand-bar, managing a smile. 'I'm fine. I feel the same as you about getting away for a while! Who wants road anyway?'

They bumped and swayed down a broad stony path and it petered out to a track. They crossed a bridge, turned down another rocky slope, and, against the stark beauty of the country, a spread of green around the village emerged, made possible by the simplest of very effective irrigation systems. A water channel ran parallel to the river, from which the village and its small cluster of houses could draw off water for its own fields.

The village itself comprised three small shops and a tea-house. Piers parked the Land Rover in the shade of a mulberry tree and leapt out, looking around him. Louise followed, tying a scarf round her head to ward off the sun. Her long cotton dress hardly moved in the still air, as she looked at the open-fronted shops. 'It doesn't seem too hopeful,' she said as Piers joined her, and they stared at the display of empty wooden boxes.

Inside one of the shops, an old, long-bearded Afghan gave them a solemn bow, and Piers told him what they wanted. The man immediately shook his head, then burst into a stream of words which Louise guessed did not hold out a lot of hope. Piers answered him in Farsi, but it gained no response. 'Blast!' Piers said, turning away. 'I can't get him to budge. I don't think he believes we're from the clinic——'

'Can I help you, my friend?'

Commander Anjum was strolling towards them from the house nearby in which they knew he was occasionally billeted. His smile was warm, and Louise looked once again at the quick, intelligent brown eyes, the first thing that had held her interest when they had first met. He had a long, well-shaped nose, and the brow of a thinker rather than a man of action. Although he was only twenty-nine, his authority, his quiet maturity, made him feared and respected by his men. That day he wore a combat suit, his face rather pale-skinned beneath a trim beard. His proud bearing revealed an innate awareness of the great responsibility he bore in leading the fight for his country. But now he was throwing his head back with laughter, as Piers greeted him soberly saying,

'I'm afraid we're in trouble, Commander. We're rapidly running out of food, and the old man here seems unwilling to help.'

'He will change his mind—you will see.' With a few well-chosen words the Commander brought a smile to the old shopkeeper's face. With another bow the man led Piers and Louise to a storehouse behind the shop where they were given a choice of potatoes, onions, tomatoes and fruit. There was meat—in small quantities, for there was no refrigeration—rice and wheatflour, tea and raisins.

Piers let out a low whistle. 'Would you believe it?'

'Let's hope the money goes round!' Louise laughed, watching the shopkeeper do his arithmetic after they'd made their purchases. A figure was named and Piers immediately shook his head fiercely, grabbing Louise's arm in an effort to lead her away.

'But, Piers, we've no choice!'

'Be patient,' Piers muttered, 'he'll come round.'

He did. The shopkeeper arrived at another figure by the time they reached the exit. At that point the Commander returned, and the Afghan immediately adopted a subservient atitude, bringing the price down for a third time, then everyone was satisfied.

The Commander grinned. 'Call on me or my lieutenants any time, Doctor, please remember that.'

They thanked him profusely. Louise was most impressed, realising she had hardly known the man until now. Previously he had been simply the figurehead who had brought them through hardships to safety. Now she was convinced he possessed far greater depths as a man of honour.

Piers was still concerned about the food. 'We certainly appreciate everything you've done, Commander,' he said warmly. 'We'll do exactly as you say should we run into difficulties again.'

The Commander's English was excellent, with an attractive French accent, but as he spoke his smile was rueful. 'Be on your guard, Piers—the old man is a wily one! But contact us if you need to. We will not see you starve, believe me!'

Piers nodded, his dark, handsome looks vibrant with good health, in comparison with the war-weary man standing before him. 'Many thanks for helping, anyway, sir.'

The Commander studied them both briefly, his bright eyes astute. 'I was educated in Paris, and have been to London more than once recently, and he thanks *me!*' He threw up his hands in mock despair. 'It is *we* who are indebted to you for leaving your civilised world to come out here and help my people—do not forget that. *Au revoir!*' He smiled, giving them a smart salute, then turning from them as if recalling the multitude of things that awaited his attention. As he disappeared into his mud-walled dwelling, already a jeep had raced to a stop outside, and several grim-faced Mujaheddin joined him.

Before leaving the village, Piers and Louise had cups of deliciously cool green sweet tea in the tea-house, and were even offered a bag of sweet biscuits. They shared them out with great solemnity, making sure there were enough left for the team to share when they got back. Idly, they talked in general of plans, possibilities, then fear. . .Piers' worries were still getting to him. 'It's all very well our feeling smug that we've renewed food stocks for a while, but there are medical supplies too. I have this constant nagging worry that they're going to run out before we leave. Although they assured me in Paris that plans were afoot to fly more out. . .' He shook his head. 'I wonder. At times it's as if we're on the edge of the world.'

'Things certainly seem far from easy, despite the Soviet withdrawal,' Louise pondered with a frown.

'Well, all isn't lost. We might as well go now.' Piers got smartly to his feet, his height and stature against the sunlight giving him a look of complete invincibility as they went back to the Land Rover. As they set off again, she wondered why such a random thought should cross her mind, and concluded that it must still be the unspoken fear: just how vulnerable they would all be without him.

They had driven about halfway on the return journey. In the distance, meadows lay bright with blue and yellow Alpine flowers, and cornflowers in abundance looked as if they'd been freshly enamelled. Piers was whistling away happily to himself, then he said, 'This humidity's terrible. Have you noticed the haze over the sun suddenly?'

'Could be a storm brewing,' Louise remarked.

'I'll step on it. You may be right.'

As they rattled along, red-veiled women crouched in small groups harvesting the corn with sickles, little boys splashed in the shallows of the river, a dog leapt and bounded after a butterfly. The Land Rover raced over the narrow bridge again, and onwards through a stream that crossed the road. Then, without warning, the engine shuddered spasmodically. A large bang emitted from somewhere beneath the car and they stopped dead. Louise groaned inwardly.

Piers jumped out. 'Damn!' He sluiced water over the bonnet, which only brought on a sinister hiss. 'Switch the engine on again!' he instructed impatiently. But nothing happened; only a metallic cough and a brief poltergeist-like knocking was heard. In front of them the road climbed towards the clouds at the top of the pass. The sky was darkening with menacing slowness. Piers looked offended at the turn of events. 'Not only have we hit a rock and clobbered the sump, but the engine's overheated as well!'

'Surely you could have at least seen what was happening to the sump by the oil gauge? There's no need to sound so surprised!' said Louise, fretful with the heat.

Piers left the bonnet up and came round to the passenger side, wiping his hands on an oily cloth, explaining with stony politeness, 'For your information, the oil gauge, by the look of it, hasn't worked for months! As for my sounding surprised, I thought this. . .this heap could take more than twenty-five miles an hour just occasionally!'

Louise got out of the vehicle, her eyes on the bruised sky. 'Well, what are we going to do now?'

'You tell me!' he snapped suddenly. 'One thing's certain—we're not going to hold the traffic up, are we?'

'I suppose we could walk back, and collect the supplies later.'

'Approximately twenty-five kilometres? You've got to be joking, when we need to get back quickly to do our spell of duty.'

A few spots of rain splashed down; the clouds had banished the blue sky and the sun, leaving the atmosphere oppressively hot. A dull, persistent boom of distant thunder rolled lazily around the mountain peaks.

Piers ran a hand over his chin, staring into space. 'Just a minute. I wonder. . .' He flung the door of the Land Rover open, and from the front picked up a piece of equipment. 'Radio telephone,' he told Louise, already trying to call up the hospital. 'I'd quite forgotten Dr Colbert said that one of the other doctors had fitted it up for them. Although obviously it hasn't been used too often. . .'

Louise listened to the hollow crackling and squawking that came from the instrument, then followed by a dismembered voice. And from the satisfied beam that eventually spread across Piers' face, he'd made contact.

'Hi, Alain. Yes, Piers! We've broken down, I'm afraid. If you can get someone to come out with the necessary to repair the sump—not forgetting the oil—

we should be able to get back OK. We've got the food, yes. Sure, that's fine.' Then his face puckered. 'Oh, hell, really? How bad is it? Right! Well, it looks pretty grim here too. Tell Jan to make it out here as soon as he can, anyway. Of course I realise it'll be on horseback!' He sighed with exasperation. 'If at all possible perhaps you could contact one of the Muj to see if there's any kind of vehicle going spare to help us out. Well, do what you can.' Briefly, Piers gave details of their exact location, and, after exchanging a few further details, cut out.

For a second he sat staring disconsolately into space.

'What's the matter?' queried Louise. 'What's happened back there?'

He shook his head slightly, as if just remembering her presence. Slowly he returned the RT to its place. 'Apparently the storm's already broken at Zari. They're dealing with one heck of a flood, water everywhere. God knows when they'll be able to get out here to us. There's nothing else for it—we'll just have to stay put, that's all.'

As if to confirm his words, thunder crashed mightily, then grumbled away; all the while the sky was now becoming as black as night with terrifying speed.

'We can't stay with the Land Rover!' exclaimed Louise, as lightning split the sky, making her jump nervously. Rolls of thunder exploded one after the other, as together, in a rising wind, they battened down the Land Rover as best they could.

Hardly able to stand upright with the sudden force of the wind, Piers shouted, 'Come on, we'll try and head for the caves!'

CHAPTER SIX

PIERS grabbed Louise's hand, and together they ran for shelter as brilliant lightning jagged down the sky. Louise's feet hardly touched the ground in an effort to keep up with the fast stride of Piers' long legs. Like athletes they sprinted across the rough, uneven land, slipping and skidding in an attempt to reach some kind of cover before the heavens really opened and the deluge fell.

Louise's hand dropped from his. 'I. . .can't run any more!' she panted, falling to her feet.

Piers was at her side, hauling her up. 'Yes, you can! Come on, give me your hand,' he shouted against the tumult above, and pointed to a track up the mountain-side. 'It's not far now!'

Her legs were buckling, but Piers would not let go her hand. He put an arm round her, all but dragging her up the slope. Torrents of heavy rain fell, soaking them both to the skin, and still they ran.

Louise's mind was in a whirl. After the long trek from Peshawar she was not yet back to a normal state of fitness that left any energy to spare. Tiredness was her enemy when there was so much to be done at the hospital, and, it seemed, never enough sleep for any of them.

Now Piers' grasp tightened on her as they toiled up the narrowing track. To their right, rain sent a cascading, crystal-clear waterfall tumbling over granite rocks, and trees overhung the water's edge. On their left the mountain rose formidably, but a wide cave entrance suddenly revealed itself by the wild wind frenziedly blowing the sparse greenery—only to close over again from sight the next second.

'In here, Louise! Quick!' He held back the scrubby

branches just long enough to allow them both into the
mouth of the cave, the trees already swaying to the
ground and back in their torment.

With groans of relief they stepped out of the long
silver rods of rain and into the dry, musty shadows, both
leaning against the cave wall gasping for breath, still
holding hands, unable to speak. Thunder continued to
roar like a monster losing sight of its plaything, lightning
lit up their shelter with shapeless patterns on the wall, as
gradually the two of them regained a degree of normality
and grinned at each other.

'How on earth did you know this place was here,
Piers?'

He laughed, exultantly almost, running a wet hand
over his face, shaking his hair as if just stepping from a
shower. 'I didn't. It was sheer good luck and a little local
knowledge!' He smiled back. He was still breathing
heavily, strong teeth even whiter in the dim light. 'Let's
just hope our Land Rover isn't swept away on a sudden
flood of water. Anything can happen in this country!'

'I quite believe it!' Louise was lifting the hem of her
long cotton dress and wringing the water out. 'While
we're here stuck in this cave for goodness knows how
long, our hospital's likely to go floating down the river
like Noah's Ark.'

His quiet chuckle echoed around the walls just as a
further bolt of thunder sent them of one accord deeper
inside the cave. Large boulders lay scattered about, and
underfoot was a wide ledge, dry and covered with early
summer weeds that ran alongside a fast-flowing subter-
ranean stream. Piers eyed the water sceptically. 'I prefer
not to be here if that overflows; on the other hand, it's
very useful, I suppose, during the heat.'

'How long are we planning on staying?' Louise
quipped, hugging her torso and trying to stop herself
from shivering, the thin wet dress clinging to every line
of her figure. Piers' baggy trousers and long shirt were
equally wet, but only seemed to emphasise his manliness.

She hadn't given a thought to her own shapely contours, revealed as if she wore nothing at all. A wave of shivers served to stress the fact, as she added, 'I mean, shall we call for the manager?'

Piers smiled, admiring the girl for the way she was trying to keep things light. This was something he'd been grateful for on their outward trip to Zari. Languidly he took off his shoes and tipped the water out into the stream, his eyes amused. 'Well, we don't know his name, do we?'

'True. Perhaps we'd better give it a miss, then!' Her teeth had begun to chatter in the cold, stony cathedral of their shelter.

He was standing, arms folded across his chest. 'As soon as I can, once the rain eases, I'll take another look at the vehicle and see if there's a repair on the sump job I've missed. Trouble is, it's already afternoon and the light's practically gone now.'

'Well, at least you made contact with the team—that's one thing to be thankful for.'

She felt his eyes upon her as he said quietly, 'Stop worrying about the team, and come and sit down on this boulder.'

She sat beside him, wanting to giggle at the incongruity of the situation, yet irritated at the cool, calm way he was taking it. Her mind still dwelt on the risk of running out of food at the clinic, and Commander Anjum's kindness when for him there were such larger issues at stake. Being out here in the desolation of a mountain thunderstorm seemed irresponsible in the extreme. . . She looked at Piers as he leaned back against the wall, a relaxed smile across his face together with a laid-back nonchalance that help would turn up some time. The words leapt from her mouth almost before they were formed, as she said curtly, 'I suppose you're enjoying this state of affairs?'

For a minute he looked startled, then said easily, 'It could be much worse.'

'I suppose it *is* the sump that's gone? We didn't just run out of petrol?' she suggested crisply.

'Wouldn't think so. When an irresistible force meets an immovable object, there's usually an obvious result,' he answered with deadly calm. 'And I didn't organise the thunderstorm either.'

She felt a pang of remorse, but didn't say so. 'Well, we certainly seem to have got more than we bargained for today, apart from the food.'

He shrugged. 'Despite everything, the change must be good for us. Look upon it as a morale-boosting therapy for the staff, and we're the lucky ones! After all, being confined to an eighteen-hour day doing hospital work isn't that funny. Besides, it gets to be monotonous. I shall register my disapproval!'

'Rather soon for us to start complaining to our union, wouldn't you say?'

'You're probably right. Talking of long hours, what did you make of Alain's odd turn-about the other day over that appendix job?' Piers asked, serious suddenly.

'I think you did the right thing.' Louise raised her voice above another reminder of the battle of the elements. 'You've since kept him off surgery on purpose. In other words, marking time to see how he shapes up.'

'Smart girl!' he mocked laconically. 'But who would have thought that beneath Alain's outwardly easygoing exterior lurked a personality that suffered such pangs of. . .indecision? To me, it doesn't seem to tie up.'

'With what?'

'His usual affable manner. . .his personality.'

'Given strange and anxious circumstances, any one of us can act out of character. I don't have to tell *you* that. I think you're taking the mickey.'

He grinned. 'I like hearing your views—really!'

Her shivering had stopped for a while, and she remembered she'd not taken the scarf from her head. Removing it sent a shower of raindrops falling from her hair, yet its sheen was like a shaft of golden sunlight in the dim interior. She draped the scarf on the rock beside her.

Piers watched her, saying nothing, but then he placed his warm, strong hands over her cold ones. She was grateful for it, but almost immediately tried to move her hands away from him—which only served to make him tighten his hold on her. 'Don't be so coy, Louise! The idea is that I try to keep you warm. I don't want a pneumonia case on my hands in this place, and neither am I trying to ravish you!'

She glanced away from him so that he should not see the colour that rushed to her cheeks. She said coldly, 'I guess from the male point of view that wouldn't be too far from your mind, though.'

'How can I deny such a possibility?' His damp hair had sent a lock falling to his brow, and a small cleft appeared to one side of his mouth as his eyes twinkled.

'I didn't say there was a possibility. I meant it was probably in your subconscious—there's a subtle difference. Which in my generosity gives you the benefit of the doubt.'

'So you're quite sure it's not a conscious thought on my part? I'm flattered.' He smiled wryly.

Louise didn't answer, but tossed her long hair back over her shoulders. The sudden movement caused the uplift of her breasts to thrust against the drying cotton of her dress.

Piers removed his hands from hers, his mouth tightening. 'Such wayward thoughts are dangerous, as I've learned from bitter experience.'

Louise gave a teasing smile. 'Oh, yes, I remember! All those lovely ladies you know in Paris!'

His brow clouded. 'Ladies, you say? I wonder.'

'Are you married, Piers?' she asked, no longer caring about protocol.

'I was, a long time ago, and the most miserable two years of my life it was too. Youth sends us a little mad, I think. Still, that's all finished and done with now.' For a

moment his guard was down, and it was as if he was
suddenly annoyed with himself. She was sure of it when
he said shortly, 'And you, Louise? We've time on our
hands, so what about your private life that so far you've
been so reluctant to discuss?'

She'd made a mistake in taking the lead in this
conversation, and she writhed inwardly, not wanting to
think of her misfortune, the bitter hurt buried deep
inside which had so nearly finished her but for a vein of
iron will she hadn't known she possessed. Now she gave
a casual laugh. 'I'm sure you wouldn't find my affairs at
all interesting, Piers. Quite prosaic, really.'

'Could it be perhaps that you're one of those rare
species these days. . .of innocence?'

'You'd really like to know?' she parried, suddenly
seeing Raymond in her flat, his long, intelligent face
close to hers, the curved, sensuous lips pleading to share
her bed. Loving him as she had done, she had given in,
and for weeks had felt renewed, adored, beloved. Plans
for the wedding had been going ahead, their jobs keeping
them apart when she had had to do night turns at the
hospital. But, once they had been back together again,
for Louise the world had remained firmly, wonderfully
in its place. She had barely noticed Raymond's changing
attitude towards her, the sudden excuses not to dine
together, the occasional weekend so often talked about
but never happening. Still she had lived in a joyousness
which had excluded all else. People, her friends, family,
had begun to talk. Raymond had been seen out with a
dark-haired, vibrant girl with whom he'd worked, a
barrister in training herself. The girl's father had been a
famed judge, and therefore Raymond had wanted no
gossip to touch the family. . .

Louise's thoughts passed to her present situation; to
this day in this beautiful country. . .and all the while
Piers Morell, a strange man, as enigmatic as the country
in which they found themselves, waiting for her reply.
She sat beside him, legs crossed, arms tightly hugged

around her rib-cage as if to prevent the flow of words from her; words that even at this moment still had the power to send her to pieces. She tilted back her head suddenly, caught the concerned, slightly quizzical expression in his eyes, and said quietly, 'Maybe one day I'll explain. But innocence. . .' She paused, as if trying to release the smouldering hurt with words, open the wound to free the poison lodged there. 'Naïveté, blind loyalty and belief would be better.'

She looked at him, the eyes that had never left her face, the graceful strength of his body leaning slightly forward, wanting only to catch the soft nuance of her words. It was rather as if she were talking to herself. 'Innocence. . .' she murmured, shaking her head. 'Surely sexual innocence is impossible when one's in love. But open-hearted candour and a belief in another person—now that could be innocence. If you mean that, then yes, the word fits.' She broke off, her mind delving too deep for comfort. She had almost forgotten the presence of the man at her side, and he had the capacity to encourage such outpourings by saying very little himself. She was almost angry; this was not a confessional!

Piers took her hand silently, pressing his lips to it and gazing at her from beneath his brows before letting it go. 'I want to hear nothing from you, Louise, that gives you hurt.'

The touch of his hand, the brush of his lips, had sent an alien warmth coursing through her. His closeness, the moment of deep understanding between them, seemed to draw all common sense from her. She deplored his arrogance, the confident charm, the charisma he so obviously practised in Parisian drawing-rooms. Yet she sensed he was far more than the man she saw on the surface. He was all men, both good and bad, and a war raged within her against falling prey to the wavelets of attraction from him that seemed to beckon. She could see from the dark intensity of his eyes that he knew her interest was aroused, and, as she turned to make an idle, throwaway remark, a crash of thunder reverberated around the thick age-old walls of the cave in the most horrendous fashion, extracting a wail of fear from her as simultaneously she realised she had flung herself into Piers' arms. They stood up in unison as if bracing themselves for flight, while Louise clutched him in abject terror as the echoing explosions pounded wildly through the rock chamber in which they were imprisoned.

Her screams were muffled against his chest, her whole body shaking with fright, as it seemed the end of the world had come.

He held her to him, body to body, warmth to warmth, his quiet strength protecting her with as much surety as the antiquity of the solid mass about them. He reached up a hand to stroke the back of her head to soothe her trembling, all the while murmuring words of comfort that seemed to flow over her like balm, as at the same time the crescendo diminished, lessened, then silenced, to fade away into the distance like a stricken animal. At length tranquillity filled her with an arcane restfulness impossible to describe. She simply knew that her entire body had gone through a massive trauma with the jilting, and this now culminated in her terror with the storm. She was left with a serenity she thought never to know again. Bitterness, disillusionment, shattered pride, all faded for a while into the background.

'Louise, Louise, don't be afraid,' Piers was pleading. 'You mustn't be. . .We're safe now, it's all over. . .You're not alone, you know.'

The deep and gentle resonance of his voice came through to her, the tenderness there as she turned her face up to speak, hesitating, for it was like returning from a long journey, and finding peace in the arms of a stranger.

'Piers. . .' she whispered. 'Thank you. You must think I'm crazy. . . I'll be OK now, I mean it, honestly.'

His arms were still locked around her, his muscular

frame against hers, although less tense now that Thor, the mythical thunder-god, had retreated from battle. As their eyes met it was as if Piers hadn't heard her. His expression was still one of compassion. One hand gentled the soft curve of her cheek, his fingers splayed across her brow, her cheekbones, the long, beautiful tresses of hair lying damply on her shoulders. His voice was low, a deep tremor revealing the sensitivity of his thoughts. 'Yes, Louise, I know that you mean what you say. I'm sure you're right. At last I'm beginning to see and know the real you.'

There was a gentle humour in his eyes, and far more than she could define in the rapidly fading light. All she was certain of was that she had to shake herself from this dangerously submissive mood. The tumult of the storm had caused a far greater tumult within, one that had been an upheaval of her senses as well as a cleansing of the misery. And yet why? As if in answer to the unspoken question, Piers' lips brushed hers. Another tremor went through her, but she disregarded it. She smiled at him, the smile of friends who had come through danger together, back to safety. 'You know, what you said just now about the real me. I sometimes wonder if there is one. . .' she murmured softly. 'How often do you think we change in a lifetime? Even poor old Alain's wrestling with the same thing.' She stirred in his arms, the calm of the world outside silent now but for the frenetic gushing of the stream and the loud gurgle of new rivulets as they converged busily, reminding her of her and Piers' commitments.

Piers was very still as he held her, reluctant to let the slender vibration of her body go from him. He also knew that she must be chilled to the bone. He raised one eyebrow imperceptibly at her comment. 'I think such changes come about by the very nature of things, rather depending upon the people we meet in certain sets of circumstances. It must have to, surely.' He glanced down at the thin material of her dress, still damp enough to outline the tantalising curve of her breasts, the perfect symmetry of thigh and legs, and Piers wondered yet again who the man was who could have been such a fool as to cause the anguish in her eyes that he'd recognised so many times. But now he was concerned about her in a different way. 'No more philosophising, my girl. You're shivering again, and I'm going to light a fire somehow.'

'Great! I'll help.'

'You stay there. The storm hasn't quite played itself out yet, I can hear it in the distance. But with luck I'll be able to grab a few of those branches and make some sort of a fire with them for a start. Maybe you could find a collection of stones here to keep it contained.'

They each went about their tasks, Piers returning with an armful of tree wood that had been hurled down, and some of which had been flung fortuitously inside the mouth of the cave itself. Louise gathered flat, smooth brown stones and made a circle of them. 'Matches!' she groaned, looking round in despair.

'Don't be defeatist! Travelling the world teaches self-preservation!' He patted his pocket. 'I'm never without them!'

While the rain continued to fall, they knelt down and snapped the branches into even smaller twigs, piling them criss-cross-wise with great care. 'All we need now is. . .this!' From the same pocket Piers produced a rather damp shopping-list written hours ago. 'And a great deal of optimism!'

It took several matches before a thin, wavering spiral of grey smoke slowly ignited the wood from the paper. Triumph was in the shape of a bright orange flame that suddenly rose from the centre of the fire like a genie, sending its light into the shadowy corners of their shelter. 'Wha-hoa!' Piers yelled. 'We've made it!'

Louise clapped her hands in delight. 'Terrific! All mod cons, would you believe it? Do you think we have enough wood to keep it going?'

'Certain of it.' He glanced across the fire at her, a
devilish grin on his features. 'Come on, then.'

'What?'

'Take your dress off, and anything else that's still
wet!'

'In here? You must be joking! What about you, then?'

'Doesn't apply to me. A sultry, warm-blooded creature
like myself has an inner fire for such occasions!'

She laughed at his nonsense, adding more twigs to the
already blazing fire that spat and crackled as she smiled
across the leaping flame at Piers. His face was bathed in
the soft light, planes and contours perfect, yet etched
with a certain hardness. His eyes too told of driving
ambition, even ruthlessness. The broad smile seemed
devoid of any inner happiness, and still she wondered
about him and why he had never married again.

Warmed through with the heat that had settled into
brightly glowing embers, and not too voracious an
appetite for refuelling, they sat back to back for a while,
close to it, talking fitfully of clinic affairs, conversation
on deeper things discarded for the need to satisfy with
more creature comforts. Louise sighed, feeling the strong
ripple of muscles down Piers' back, as she said wistfully,
'Do you happen to be hungry, by any chance?' She felt
his voice vibrate against her back.

'Well, now that you mention it. . .'

'Just think of all the lovely food in the vehicle!' she
said dreamily. 'Good thing most of it's in covered tins—
that's another of the very useful hints Dr Colbert gave
us. Tins guard against insects, weather and humans!'

'What a wise young woman you are!' he teased,
suddenly swinging round, causing her to sway backwards. He caught her playfully, then left one arm across
her shoulders as they sat together in friendly silence,
seeing pictures in the fire. Louise knew she should move
from him, that the unexpected show of comradeship was
just and only that.

He was gazing thoughtfully into the fire, and, feeling

suddenly over-conscious of him, she moved and began to run her fingers through her hair in an effort to dry it. As she swept it up and over her head so that its abundance swung down in front of her face, the firelight brought it to life with a thousand pin-points of gold light. . .

'Let me do that for you,' Piers offered.

She threw her hair back, sudden defiance surging through her. 'No, it's only damp now. . . I——'

Her protests went unheard. 'Turn with your back to the fire and lean on your elbows, and allow Luigi to attend to one of his best clients!'

'You're a fool!' She laughed, doing as she was told and wondering why. But she felt a shiver of excitement go through her as his hands, gentle but firm, began to move slowly with rhythmic, sensual movements from the very top of her head right to the very tip of her hair. It hung like a bright flame between them, Piers kneeling at her side, saying little, yet she could almost hear the pounding of his heart, he was so close.

His fingers ran through the luxuriant silkiness that seemed to cling as his hands moved through it, and the warmth of the fire made it shine about her head. 'Your hair's very beautiful,' he murmured suddenly, as he drew it back from her face, and she looked up at him, reflections from the fire in her eyes making them deep and lustrous as they met his. 'I feel privileged. . .' he told her with sincerity.

Louise gave a small, casual laugh, yet an undercurrent of sensual pleasure had been aroused within her at his touch. Why was she being such a fool as to be this compliant with his changing moods? Quite suddenly she moved her head from his hands, saying quickly, 'That's fine now, Piers, thanks.'

'I know it's fine, Louise,' he said gently, 'but that isn't the reason you no longer want me to touch your hair, is it?'

'Yes of course. . . I mean—er—no,' she stammered,

swaying towards him, drawn by the magic of the moment, the knowledge in his eyes that he knew what she was thinking.

His lips claimed hers, a long, long kiss of submission, one of such dizzying sensuality that it filled her senses with desire. His hands were on her shoulders, drawing her closely and intimately against him, as gently they fell back on to the carpet of weeds. Her hair spread in a burnished fan above her head, his hands cupping her face as he gazed at her, an expression of sheer wonderment crossing his features. 'Louise, how much longer did you think you could taunt me, torment me this way?'

Their bodies met, the light covering of material between them no more than another skin. Her breasts strained against him, and the touch of his hand on their pink ripeness wrung a gasp from her as his searching lips pressed hard on hers before probing deeper into the moist sweetness of her mouth. . . He caressed the slender column of her neck, the thistledown brush of his lips creating more havoc to her thudding heart than any urgent kiss of passion.

The front opening of her dress gave beneath his hands, his bent head sending a trail of butterfly kisses fluttering slowly, teasingly towards the swell of the golden velvet globes that made him raise dark, unfathomable eyes to hers, saying hoarsely, 'Do you realise just how desirable you are, Louise? How could anyone be so foolish as to. . .' He left the sentence in mid-air, somewhere in his subconscious a signal warning him not to refer to anything that could ruin such a time. His lips skimmed across the rosy-tipped breasts until with a groan of ecstasy he buried his face between the cleft of her womanly beauty. 'Louise, you're like honey,' he murmured, 'every magnificent part of you. . .'

'Piers,' she whispered huskily, 'we're mad. . . please. . .!'

But her weak protests went unheeded, and soon there was no longer even another skin between them; only the uniting of their bodies was all that mattered. For Louise, every vein, sinew and limb melted at his touch, bringing her alive, their need for each other all-encompassing. If there was any remaining resistance on her part it was forgotten as briefly, in some other universe, fire and enchantment spun madly together—until in its own time it ceased, with the contentment that follows trauma; warmth that follows cold; peace following a storm. . .

Spent, they lay in each other's arms. Louise was silent until she felt Piers' lips on her forehead. He had leaned up on one elbow, and was gazing at her.

'Piers, it was——' She knew he'd sensed she was going to say 'wrong', and he'd stopped her.

His wide shoulders shook slightly as he laughed, placing a forefinger against her lips. 'Don't say it!' He stood up, pulling her with him, tilting her chin with his hand. 'Don't start analysing. It happened. In this life it's as unpredictable as the storms around us!'

Louise made no answer, only straightened her hair and dress, moving from him. A withdrawn expression on her face was already taking the place of a radiance that had been there such a short time ago. Her mind, nevertheless, was no longer racked with anxieties, rights or wrongs, only filled with the amazing knowledge that Piers Morell had made love to her, and it was too incredible to dwell upon, let alone analyse.

He was at the mouth of the cave, surveying the rain-washed sky. The storm was over and above was an indigo canopy scattered with a million stars. He turned to her with a low laugh. 'The sky's as clear as we could wish now, and thank heaven I can just about see the Land Rover from here. I suggest I go down there and see what I can do.'

The night was once again warm and airless. There was little breeze, and the cave behind Louise smelt musty as well as smoky. While she was listening to Piers, something warm and furry had run across her foot, the returning humidity stirring the animal night-life. . . She shuddered, determined not to let him know how terrified she was of small furry creatures, whatever they were. 'I'm coming too!' she called.

'You're not. It's probably very slippery!'

'I am, and you can't stop me!'

'OK, please yourself, but be careful.'

Gingerly she followed him down, skidding in an occasional patch of mud, but on the whole the ground was drying fast and already loose stones slid ahead of her. When at last she reached the vehicle, Piers was opening tins and finding bread. Together they climbed in. He handed her a piece of the *nan*, and took a hunk of the thin, unleavened bread himself. In blissful silence they did justice to every crumb, followed by an orange each, which seemed to put new life into them.

'Survival's a funny thing, isn't it?' Louise deliberated thoughtfully. 'It means so many things.'

Piers nodded. 'Indeed. Which reminds me, I wonder if they've cleared the hospital of water yet? What a job it must have been!' He glanced through the windscreen at a huge silver moon that had just put in an appearance above the mountains. 'Good, light at last! I'll have another look at that sump now.'

Before he jumped down from the vehicle, he turned round to look at her, just the briefest glimpse in his expression of the man she'd known for such a short space of time; the one who had now vanished, and was once again Piers Morell, whom she either liked or loathed.

'Louise,' he was saying quietly, 'when we get back, things will have to carry on as usual. You do understand?' His smile swung to the side of his mouth, a combination of reserve and perhaps slight embarrassment.

She smiled back. 'As if it never happened.'

He looked relieved. 'I'm still in charge of the team whatever happens, and when we return to Zari the ethics of our profession have to be observed.'

She burst into a bubble of laughter. 'Don't be so pompous, Piers! You sound exactly like Alain, and you're not a bit like him!'

'I appreciate that, coming from you, Dr Holden!' He grinned cheekily.

She watched him clamber lithely down from the Land Rover and inspect the source of the trouble. In a sense they were two of a kind—professionalism and dedication in their work being uppermost. There was one thing of which she could be certain: whenever they worked together there would always be respect between them. That did not mean that she had given up thinking of him as the conceited, overbearing male who had infuriated her from the very first time they had met, and no doubt the situation would remain so; but she still admired him.

Three hours later, Jan arrived on horseback to repair the job that Piers, to his chagrin, had been quite unable to do. Jan set to with his tools and materials, meanwhile giving them the latest news from the hospital.

'A pretty terrible time has been had by all,' he told them wearily. 'We've managed to get most of the water out of the wards, but until tomorrow we won't know the full extent of the damage.'

Piers looked worried. 'The rest of the staff all right?' he asked, giving Jan a hand with the work.

'I suppose so. Alain didn't exert himself over-much. Oh, yes, and poor old Monique doesn't seem too well. She has some sort of stomach pain, and I told her to get off to bed. Usual women's problem, I imagine.'

'Didn't she say what it was?' Louise asked anxiously.

'Not really. She insists she'll be fine in a day or two.'

When at length the vehicle was pronounced as fit as it could ever be, they all parted company, Jan doing the return journey the way he had come, leaving Piers and Louise to get back as soon as they could to give assistance where necessary.

As the hospital came into sight, dawn was already

streaking the sky in a blaze of colour. Piers slowed the vehicle down, looking across at Louise. 'You've been very quiet,' he remarked.

She gave a wry grin. 'Of necessity, really. This is where we truly revert to type.'

He didn't smile. 'Louise, I——' He broke off, as if thinking better of what he'd been going to say, and stepped up the speed once more.

Louise pretended not to have heard him, already knowing there was a great deal of work facing them, and for the coming weeks that was all that mattered.

CHAPTER SEVEN

LATER that morning, with only the briefest claim to sleep, both Piers and Louise had discussions with the staff on the latest news as they sat over breakfast. Monique insisted that she was quite well, although Louise had had little chance to talk to her in private. After that the main topic was planning an attack of spring-cleaning on the hospital in order to be rid of any residue left from the flood-water.

An hour or so before midday, Commander Anjum arrived, having delegated a group of his men to help, including coaxing the portable generator to work again. At midday the Mullah started the call to prayer, bringing the two ranks of young men to their knees to bow and touch their foreheads in an act of worship. Thereafter they attacked the rest of the job with a will, and by early evening most things were shipshape again. Louise went into the kitchen to get the Commander a cup of tea, having made sure his men had been looked after, and found a more animated Monique already there with the same idea.

'Oh, great, Monique!' Louise smiled. 'I can leave you to look after the Commander, then—he's been a terrific help!'

'Yes, 'e 'as been telling me about 'is travels. I find 'im very nice, Louise.' Monique smiled, although she looked rather pale.

'Are you feeling better now? Jan said you've not been too well. You've had problems?'

'Don't we all! It is nothing. Period pains, I think.'

Louise was about to have her evening meal with Jan, and she made her way thoughtfully across to the table, still thinking of Monique. Jan was already seated, there having been little time recently for a communal gathering as they liked when things were less urgent. He gave a grin as she sat down, and the usual meat and rice was put in front of them.

'Hi, Jan! I hope you've got over that long horse-ride by now.'

He rubbed his seat. 'Ask me in six months!' He tucked into his meal. 'Have you recovered from your session with our boss yet?'

She laughed lightheartedly, but her stomach lurched. 'Amazing how soon one forgets cold and hunger! But I'll never forget how glad we were to see you!'

They talked shop for a while, then Jan said quietly, giving her a long stare, 'You know, you remind me of my wife, Louise.'

'Your wife, Jan? I thought you were a confirmed bachelor. All those sporting events you take part in in Stockholm and everywhere—I'd imagined that filled your life!'

'Anna does that now, but she believes that I should continue with my athletics. We married just before I left, and I miss her very much. . .'

Louise could see no likeness to herself whatsoever when Jan showed her a picture of Anna, and could only conclude that Jan was madly in love, and that all fair-haired girls had something of his wife about them. 'She's lovely; I'm sure she's very proud of you,' she said, handing back the photograph of a pretty, curly-haired girl.

'And I of her,' he said sombrely as they parted company, 'but she is such a long way away, and I don't know how she will manage.' He shrugged suddenly. 'But her parents are very rich and will probably lure her back. They do not approve of me.'

A long queue was already forming for the evening surgery. At this time of evening their patients were mostly male. In a sense the routine of the hospital organised itself.

Alain and Louise spent the first half-hour of their duty busily opening cartons containing drugs and dressings, and spreading them carefully on the table. Everything had to be accounted for. Because of dire poverty among certain village patients, it was not beyond one or two of the more unscrupulous to help themselves to anything worth bartering or selling.

A rather wild-looking character, their first patient, entered the room at the direction of one of the girl auxiliaries. He stood before them, black-eyed, bearded, hugely tall, and dressed in an array of army oddments on top of his more traditional Muslim dress, and appeared nothing less than a dubious brigand.

Alain pushed up his glasses on the narrow bridge of his rather sharp nose. 'What is the trouble?' he asked mildly.

The man jerked up his sleeve, revealing an angry-looking knife wound as dangerously close as it could be to the radial artery. After examining it, Alain appeared relieved, one of the girl interpreters translating this back to the patient. 'Fortunately for him it's only just missed the artery by centimetres. I've told him how lucky he is.'

But when the man saw Louise preparing the sterilising equipment to stitch the wound, the giant's legs gave way beneath him and he fell to the floor in a dead faint.

Alain and Louise looked at each other aghast, as simultaneously they dropped to their knees to help the man. Then their eyes met, the same thought striking them at the same time. 'He's out cold,' Louise said thoughtfully. 'It might be possible to do the job while he's like that. . .'

'Why not?' Alain said quickly. 'He's a big brute, and by the way his eyes were rolling at the sight of the hypodermic needle, I wouldn't rate our chances very high for getting anywhere near him.'

'OK,' Louise said briskly. 'I'll start suturing, and you prepare a light shot in the syringe in case he comes round sooner than we think.'

But he didn't, and they were just putting the finishing touches to the final dressing when the patient opened his eyes dazedly. He sat up, looked at his bandaged wrist with amazement, then a huge beam spread across his face as he stood up, suddenly able to speak English.

'Finished, yes? You are good! Very good!' He laughed, displaying his bandaged wound to anyone who cared to look, then disappeared.

Louise and Alain were laughing too, as Piers came in from the women's ward. 'What's the commotion out here?' he wanted to know. He grinned broadly when they told him. 'Great PR job! The man will think we have magical powers from now on and do us a bit of good!'

Louise planned on having an early night after she went off duty. It was difficult to stop thinking of her primitive bed, which to her, after being in the cave, was sheer, unadulterated luxury. She knew that Monique was doing a late shift, and so she had a little time to herself, which both girls tried to allow each other whenever possible.

That evening, while clearing up after the final surgery, Louise noticed that Varsha, another of the auxiliaries, seemed troubled and had hardly spoken a word. Her mass of tumbled brown curls tied back with a scarf, and her limpid brown eyes, made her a very attractive young girl, but so far Louise had not had a chance to say a lot to her. The girl was obviously upset, and as they collected up empty bottles and discarded paper wrappers, Louise asked, 'Do you feel all right, Varsha?'

The girl hung her head, and tears had sprung to her eyes.

'Varsha,' Louise urged, 'can I help?'

But the girl only shook her head and ran from the room. Louise did not follow. It was time for Varsha to go home to the village anyway, but she'd try and see her tomorrow. Now, after something to eat, all she could think about was going to bed and reading a book.

Several hours later she awoke with a start to hear her

name being whispered in her ear. 'Dr Holden, come quickly, it's Sister Lefarge!'

Louise staggered up, struggling into her clothes. 'What's wrong, Sabia? Is anyone with her? Tell me as we go,' she said, hurriedly slipping on her sandals and following Sabia across to the hospital. 'What happened?' she asked, catching up with the girl. 'When was it?'

'It was just before she must come off duty, Doctor, she tells me she would go outside for a moment because she has big pain. I think she is all right, but later Commander Anjum, who wanted to see one of his men, brings her in. She is in his arms, and bleeding. . .' Sabia's eyes were huge with fear and apprehension.

In the ward, behind an ancient old rattan screen, Monique lay moaning with pain. Commander Anjum was holding her hand, and he shook his head when he saw Louise. 'I came back this evening, as you know, and walking to my jeep across the compound heard what I thought was the sound of an animal. Instead. . .*mon Dieu*! It was Sister lying on the ground.' He looked devastated. 'I picked her up, not knowing what to do, and we got her on to the bed.'

Louise was flabbergasted. Her first thoughts just couldn't be true. Leading the Commander outside, and thanking him, she told him she would see him later and hurried back to Monique. The Frenchwoman was drifting in and out of her semi-conscious state, and then her face was horribly contorted with pain as she gasped, 'Louise, 'elp me. . .please! It is. . .so terrible. . .'

Swiftly Louise despatched Sabia with an urgent message for Piers to come immediately. Meanwhile Louise examined the girl as her moans renewed, her dark hair emphasising her flushed face and pain-filled eyes. To her dismay, Louise was convinced she was right with her earlier thoughts. Poor Monique was in the throes of an incomplete abortion.

She was mightily relieved to see Piers, who made the same diagnosis. Outside the screen, he said, 'The blood

loss is severe. Thank God we have some plasma. We'll
also give her pethidine hydrochloride, about a hundred
MGs to ease the pain. Then we'll get her to the op table.'

The usual preparations were made for the minor
operation as far as was possible. Alain had been fetched
and was designated to watch over Monique while she
was rendered unconscious. Piers had hardly said a word,
and, while they waited for the blood to be transfused,
Louise sensed that this emergency was not improving his
opinion of Monique. Louise recorded observations of
pulse, blood-pressure and vaginal loss.

During the entire operation Piers' words were short
and to the point. 'We must be certain that all products
of the conception are completely expelled.' A dilation
and curettage was performed, the curettings to be put
aside for examination at an appropriate time.

Still sleepy, Monique was taken back to the screened
bed, Louise staying with her until she had fully regained
consciousness. Gradually her eyes focused sleepily on
Louise, and she touched her hand. 'Sorry about this. . .
I kept 'oping I was. . .wrong. . .'

Louise smoothed her pillow, whispering softly, 'Don't
worry about anything, Monique, just have a good sleep
now and you'll be fine. Tell Sabia if you want anything.
I'm on call tonight and she'll fetch me.'

Still stunned, Louise left the ward, slipping the scarf
from her hair and glad to be outside in the night air. She
strolled across the compound, her thoughts about
Monique chasing one after the other. What would
happen now? Would Piers allow her to stay? Was it the
married man she had mentioned who had been the father
of the aborted child? With a sigh of melancholy, she
turned her eyes up to the galaxy of stars in the ink-blue
sky. We try to plan a life for ourselves, she thought,
make certain if we can that we're doing the right thing,
and then we throw it all aside for another more tempting
pathway.

She stopped suddenly, seeing Piers leaning against one

of the tree-trunks. As if in a reverie, he walked lazily towards her. 'You must have been having the same thoughts as I,' he said.

'Yes. I must say it's been a shock.'

'Whichever way you look at it, it's a disaster. To think she did the whole of that outward journey not knowing she was pregnant! The girl must be mad! I always thought there was something too carefree about her.'

'You're a man, and you *would* look at it like that! You know nothing of the circumstances and neither do I,' Louise said frostily. 'Monique's a damned good nurse, easy to get on with, and. . .well, we all have our troubles.'

'You know that's not the point! People are selected to take these jobs, required to be in good health, with no medical complications whatsoever. Even taking aspirin in my opinion's risky, if you begin to need more. We have to rely upon our own resources! That's the trouble with women coming to such a place—they're totally unreliable! It was just her luck tonight that I'd brought one or two gynae instruments with me. God, it makes me mad!'

Louise seethed, and her breath came in ragged gasps. 'You've got a nerve, talking like that! Women have done fine work all over the world in such places, and a lot of you men wouldn't be here today but for them!' she exploded. 'Did Monique let you down on the long trip out? Did she hold things up so that you and your precious time schedule was put out? No! She kept it all bottled up in her mind, coping with something which in the beginning was a man's fault anyway! It isn't a crime to fall in love with the wrong man, you know!' Her voice petered out; to her horror she realised she was having difficulty in choking back tears. She swung round on her heel, walking away from him and, without noticing, away from the compound. She felt his hand on her shoulder.

'Louise. . .Louise, I'm sorry, I'm just getting a bit

overwrought myself at the moment. OK, I take it all back about Monique, it was thoughtless of me. We'll work something out about that later.' He flung his hands out in near despair. 'But I ask you, if we, the staff, can't remain firm, how can we help the people out here?'

'I know you're thinking of Alain now as well as Monique, Piers, but we'll get through it. The villagers know we're doing all we can. We won't let them down, or ourselves!'

Piers stopped walking, his shoulders sagging wearily. 'You're right. It's just that there's so much to do here and so little to do it with. There are times when I wake up in a cold sweat wondering what the day holds and whether I'm competent enough to deal with it.'

'You know you are, Piers. I know it and so do the others. It's three in the morning and we're at just about our lowest ebb; things will look much better tomorrow. . .'

He ran a hand over his eyes. 'I hate signs of weakness, particularly in myself.'

'We wouldn't be human if it didn't happen to all of us at some time. Besides, as far as you're concerned at this moment it's tiredness, not weakness.'

He pulled his shoulders back and smiled down at her earnest face. 'You're a love, do you know that? We all need a little morale-booster now and again,' he ran a hand lightly over her cheek, 'and that's what you've just done for me.'

His fingers on her skin reminded her of another time—another place. Quickly she ignored the small tremor that went through her at his touch as she said brightly, 'That's what I like to hear! Now, seeing that I'm still on call, I'll go and make us a cup of tea before you go back to bed.

Monique was up and about again a week after resting at Piers' insistence. That morning he had been to see her, and he left her and Louise having coffee together. The two girls were still talking about the prospects of Monique being allowed to remain at Zari. Pale but bright-eyed, she gave a wry grin. 'I 'ave this feeling that Piers will be glad to see the back of me. I do not mean that in a derogatory way, but 'e'll be watching me all the time in case I am not tough enough to carry on.' She shrugged, staring across the emerald-green grass and the flowers planted by their predecessors. 'What do you think, Louise? You 'ave been quiet this morning.'

'I'm rather inclined to agree with you, Monique. Piers has said nothing to me one way or the other. But you know I'll do all I can to help if you feel you can manage to stay on.'

'I want to,' the girl said fiercely. 'I have to!'

'Have to?' Louise queried with a quick look at her. 'Why?'

'Louise, because if I am sent back to Paris, believe me, I will go to Jacques' apartment and kill 'im! I went through agonies of mind just because of 'im when we started our journey. No periods came. I tell myself it is the 'eat, the food, the exhaustion. . .Once we arrived and settled down I could 'ave killed myself, let alone 'im! Then the night the Commander found me I 'ad tried to take an overdose, not very much but enough to make me sick, and then it all began to 'appen!' Her eyes widened with the recollection. '*Mon Dieu*! Those pains, they were terrible! I will never go through such a thing again. . . Sometimes I wish Commander Anjum 'ad left me where I was.'

'Hush, don't talk like that, Monique. It may be for the best, the way it happened.'

'Maybe.' She gave Louise a discerning glance. 'I once think you 'ate all men. Now I am feeling the same. You, Louise, find it 'ard to talk about what 'appened to you, but now 'ere everybody knows about me! I 'ad no intention of being second-best to any man. Why should I care about it? But the thought of my *petit bébé*. . .' Her big eyes filled with tears.

Louise put her arm round her. 'Monique, don't cry. . .you're so brave. . .' Commander Anjum was crossing the grass at that moment, carrying a bunch of flowers, and she rose to leave. 'I think you have company, Monique. I'll get back to work now.'

Monique nodded, dabbing her eyes. 'OK, thanks, *chérie!*' She gave a watery smile as the Commander handed her the flowers.

'You are better, Monique?' he asked, waving to Louise.

Louise noticed the concern in the Commander's voice as she went back to the wards. She never ceased to be amazed at the kindness of these people; the Commander especially, with the never-ending aspects of a holy war on his mind, the wellbeing of his men, their capricious, mercurial nature and at times insane bravery.

The women's clinic that morning was as busy as ever, and Louise found it even harder without Monique's efficient assistance. Varsha was with her, and she made a mental note to find a moment with the girl to see if she was still unhappy. Since the night of Monique's trouble such things had flown from her mind.

Two days later at breakfast Piers announced that he wanted both Louise and Monique to get used to driving the Land Rover. 'Me, too, Piers?' Monique asked hopefully, 'I thought. . . I wondered. . .' Her smile was hesitant, her eyes pleased.

Piers, wearing thin jeans and a white shirt that morning, looked stern. 'It is for everyone's sake, both for the present, and. . .to whomever it may refer in the future.' He met Monique's eyes as the light went from them. 'We can never tell if we may have to move the clinic. Commander Anjum says we can't rule out such a possibility, and I want to know that any one of us can drive on this rough terrain without tipping the thing over.' He turned to Louise suddenly. 'You might as well start with me tomorrow morning, Louise.'

* * *

Next day, as a clear dawn light rose over the mountains, Alain began to arouse from his night's sleep on a stretcher-bed on the office floor. Each member of the team did a week on call in this way, with one young auxiliary nurse on night duty.

He stretched and groaned, feeling slightly stiff, yet finding his surroundings infinitely more agreeable than waking at Hélène, his wife's, side, in the mansion on the Place des Vosges. As a rich woman in her own right she had spent large sums of money on its restoration, but to Alain it meant nothing. They had married only because, as he'd subsequently discovered, his medical training had intrigued her when they had first met at one of his father's interminable business parties.

She had soon tired of him, particularly once she had learned of his father's disappointment that his only son had had no intention of carrying on the two-hundred-year-old potteries that produced world-famous *objets d'art*. That was when her own shallow love had waned for him too, until eventually they had come to lead separate lives but under one roof. Afghanistan had offered escape from all that, and himself. . .

'Hi, Alain! I'm tea-girl this morning!'

Louise appeared, as he stood up and straightened his crumpled, baggy trousers and shirt. She looked fresh and lovely clad in a long yellow Muslim dress, an embroidered goatskin jacket thrown over it to ward off the early morning chill. Now there was a real woman. . .he put on his glasses, giving her a sleepy smile of welcome. 'You're an angel, Louise!' He took the beaker from her. 'To what do I owe this honour?'

'You're in luck, Alain.' She laughed. 'I'm meeting Piers early—apparently he has to go to the village and intends getting me behind the wheel of the Land Rover. He certainly has more faith in my driving than I have!' She smiled, handing another beaker to the auxiliary from the children's ward. The girl shyly sipped it down before returning to her charges.

'You should have no worries about this morning, Louise. You strike me as the sort of girl who'll accept a challenge!'

'Challenge is right, believe me!' Louise laughed.

They sat in the doorway of the clinic basking in the warmth of early morning sun, the scenery before them breathtakingly awesome, enough to draw them together in a bond of their own insignificance. The valley lay bathed in a gentle golden warmth below the sheer peaks. Pale green fields spread before them, separated by low stone walls, and, higher up the mountain slopes, crops had been terraced with great industry. Across the river a dark green field of potatoes emerged from the gauzy mist, and a pale sky, now pearl-grey, sparkled and came alive with the radiant ascent of the sun.

Alain put his beaker aside, still staring ahead. 'Home to me is where I feel at peace,' he said quietly, 'and at this moment it's right here.'

'I agree, it's——'

But Alain cut in, not hearing, 'I'll show Hélène I'm not the person she thinks I am. All I need is space away from that mausoleum she calls home. It might have been different if we'd had children—her concentration would not then always have been directed at me. Nothing I ever do pleases her, and yet when I told her I was coming out here, she was ready with the threats and recriminations. Saying I was leaving her for good. . .' He threw up his hands suddenly. 'Perhaps I am, Louise.' He brought his gaze back to her. 'Forgive me for talking this way. I cannot remember when I last unburdened myself to a friend.' Again he glanced away from her, saying quietly, 'In fact, to me you are more than that.'

Her heart went out to him, and hurriedly she tried to brush aside the implication of his words. 'It's natural to feel that way in a closed community, Alain. You'll most probably find that once you return to Paris again your wife will realise what a good husband she's spurning.'

Alain stood suddenly, his face already withdrawn into

the smiling lines that seemed permanently etched there. 'Forget the whole conversation, Louise! I had no right to talk to you this way, but just occasionally it helps to allow one's private thoughts to spill over. . .'

There was no chance to say more. Piers was walking across the compound towards them, and with his long, easy gait he reached them in seconds. His expression was introspective as he acknowledged Louise, and addressed Alain. 'Hi, Alain—any problems during the night?'

'The two kiddies in for observation have fairly high temps and the usual colds. I'll include it in my report. Let's hope it's not serious.'

'Anything I can get you in the village?'

'I've heard there's an old Afghan character who claims to be a hairdresser. You could tell me if he's still in business!' Alain grinned, pushing a hand across his thin hair.

'Right! Come on, Louise. Won't be too long, Alain!'

They set off in the Land Rover, Louise as yet still in the passenger seat. Piers glanced across at her, and her heart leapt at the closeness of him. When it did this she was always furious with herself. She tried hard to keep their association on a professional level, but it did not get any easier. He was bare-headed, dressed in a cool white European shirt, unbuttoned down to the waist, sleeves rolled, thin Afghan trousers that pulled tightly across his thighs as he handled the driving-wheel, profile proud in concentration, wide, well-shaped lips and strong jaw indicating far more. The words 'Kara Kush' came to her, meaning 'The Eagle'. One of the Mujahedin men had told her the words when they had seen eagles in flight on the journey. She had forgotten it until now, and quite suddenly in her subconscious, that, she decided, would be her name for Piers. To her he was the aloof, enigmatic male who needed no one. Lately she had sensed more than ever that she had been added to his list of female conquests, and that that was all it had meant to him. Occasionally she thought she'd seen a glimmer of admiration in his eyes for her, but she was probably quite wrong. Nevertheless, in a way it was helping her overcome the bitterness of the past, taking all her determination and forcefulness to ensure that she did not make the same mistake twice. There was no chance of that with Piers Morell, but it kept her on her toes for when they all returned to their former way of life.

'You slept well?' he was asking pleasantly.

'Yes, now that Monique's back. The nights she was bedded on the ward, I missed her very much.'

'You both get on quite well together?'

'Right from the start. By the way, Piers, have you made up your mind yet about her going back?'

'No, there are other more important issues at the moment.'

'Do let her stay, Piers.'

'Louise, I shall make a decision in my own time!' he snapped.

She hung on to her temper, noticing the nerve that worked at his temple. 'Yes, I do realise that.'

'Good. Now perhaps we can get on with your driving prowess.'

'I have no driving prowess! I've only recently passed my test at home.'

'In that case all the better. You need to handle as many different vehicles as you can, especially if you intend travelling abroad in your future career.'

'I should think that goes without saying,' she retorted smartly, as they bumped down the stony path towards the river bridge. But to her surprise, instead of crossing to make for the village, he swung the vehicle off the track and stopped.

Louise gulped. 'I don't have to take this heap to the village, do I?' she asked, although she was more than a little relieved that he'd driven over most of the snakelike bends in the road.

He hadn't answered, but stared through the windscreen as if trying to make up his mind about something. When he turned to her, his eyes were unsmiling. 'No, I don't want to push you into driving until you really feel you can cope. I'm afraid I used that partly as an excuse to get away so that I could talk to you—there's little privacy at the clinic.' He heaved a drawn-out sigh, one hand still on the driving-wheel.

'It's Alain. Have you had any further impressions about him, his work as well as his attitude?'

An immediate pang of anxiety for Alain went through her, having just that morning heard about his home life. 'There's been nothing more specific,' she said blandly, overlooking the small irritations she'd experienced when Alain had seemed to have a habit of doing the least possible work when they had been taking clinics together. 'It's taking him time to adapt, coming out here and realising what we're up against.'

He listened keenly to what she said, then relaxed back into his seat. 'I'm in one devil of a dilemma! It's up to me, of course, if I retain him. But if things are going to get sticky or we're in an emergency of some kind, I have no real faith in him. On the other hand, we'd have to wait for a replacement if I asked for one. I just don't know the answer!' He clenched a fist. 'The weird thing is, I can sense that he's not pulling his weight, yet so far there's only been that one incident when he opted out of the appendix removal.'

Louise wrestled with her knowledge of Alain's unhappy marriage. Should she tell Piers what she knew and so contribute to wrecking the only peace of mind the man might have ever had since meeting his wife? It would be on her conscience for the rest of her life, and his might be ruined because of it. The cost seemed too high. 'He's so willing to fall in with everyone,' she heard herself murmur.

'I know that,' Piers said impatiently. 'He's a good doctor in his normal surroundings, but let's face it, when it comes to imagination and improvisation he has very little going for him.'

Louise remained silent.

Piers gave her a hard look. 'OK, Louise, I can see you're finding it hard to speak out against him. Perhaps there's more to this than I realised after all. Funny how one rarely sees what's going on under one's nose!'

'I shall treat that remark with the contempt it deserves, Piers,' she said, anger welling up. 'This one incident doesn't justify a man's losing his job. If this had happened at home, he'd have been given a medical check-up and advised to take a week's leave pending results.'

Piers had set the vehicle in motion, hurling it across the bridge to the village. 'Yes, yes, I know all about that,' he shouted above the racket they were making, 'but we're not at home, are we, and you haven't got to make the decision! I was mad enough to expect some sort of help from you!'

They lurched into the village, arriving with a squeal of brakes. Piers mumbled that he had to see the Commander, and Louise spent some time talking to the local children. When he returned, it seemed that that too had been unsatisfactory. 'He wasn't there,' he told her brusquely.

'We haven't enquired about the hairdresser,' she ventured, as he swung one leg up into the Land Rover, and started the engine impatiently.

'To hell with the hairdresser!' He screwed up his eyes to stare through the windscreen. 'The Commander left his apologies. Apparently there's been some kind of ambush up in the mountains, and quite a few of his men have been wounded. We have to get back as quickly as we can.' He glanced up at the sky. 'There's likely to be retaliation in some form between government troops and the rebels, so just keep a look out.'

'Right. Presumably we'll be getting the casualties.'

'That's it! And if that bloody Alain doesn't shape up in this situation, I'll take him back myself!'

Louise breathed a sigh of relief. Alain had been reprieved once again—Monique too, with luck.

A familiar sound, low and menacing, curtailed further discussion. The sudden staccato rat-tat-tat of machine-gun fire caused Piers to stand on the brakes. 'Out! Quick! Keep down and run!'

He took her hand, and this time they were running for their lives, not to escape a deluge of rain. As they flung themselves down and flattened their faces in the cool, friendly grass, rockets exploded from the ridge of the mountains, making a wicked crack as they were fired, a short, sharp retort and puffs of smoke appearing as they struck home.

Piers had both arms round Louise, and one *pattu* over them both. Louise was too scared to breathe. A helicopter suddenly appeared in the azure sky, all the more frightening for its slow, deliberate flight. It unleashed a pair of bombs, throwing up clouds of dust and smoke in the distance, the explosions reverberating off the sides of the valley before silence gradually returned. When they raised their heads, the first thing they saw was a steady plume of grey smoke rising lazily up into the sky from the direction of Zari.

'Oh, no,' Piers muttered. 'Despite ten years of war *and* a Russian withdrawal, the country's still this divided. Come on, we must get back. Heaven knows what we'll find!' For a very brief second, as they disentangled, their eyes met; Louise could feel his soft breath fanning her face as he spoke, and she could smell fresh soap and grass on his skin. Their eyes locked.

With her heart pounding, Louise flicked a blob of mud from his chin. 'If we're going back on duty, we might as well look the part.' She laughed, standing up and brushing herself down. Piers grinned as they hurried back to the Land Rover, each silent now, wondering what they were going to find.

CHAPTER EIGHT

As THEY arrived at the clinic, smoke rose from several dwellings nearby, and one of the three buildings, including the office and stores containing old stretchers and walking equipment, had been damaged. Apart from that, four male casualties had suffered minor burns, received in their enthusiastic efforts to help put out the fire.

'Thank heaven our drugs cupboard's still intact!' Piers said, looking around at the wet debris of charred and smouldering wood that was everywhere.

Jan's blackened face split into a grin. 'We'll soon get this cleared up, Piers. The funny thing is, half the patients suddenly left their beds and gave all the help they could. We were so lucky—I believe several people were killed in more isolated spots.'

Alain and Monique were busily organising refreshments for the helpful patients, and preparing a check on each one. Alain scratched his head. 'We are so fortunate, considering what could have happened. . . But. . .'

'But what?' Piers demanded sharply. 'Is there something else?'

''Fraid so. There are at least thirty serious Mujaheddin casualties in two lorries on their way here, and that's apart from the walking wounded.'

Louise was already scooping up all the medical cartons she could see to prevent more water getting in them. 'OK, let's get on with it, then!'

From then on Louise hardly remembered the days that followed. Routine hospital work with outpatients was suspended while rebel troops were attended to. Serious cases were put on the men's ward, while the few existing patients were either prematurely discharged or placed temporarily in a primitive area.

They worked on a rota basis as usual but with less rest, Louise and Jan alternating with both Alain and Piers. Monique, insisting she was quite fit again, was put in charge of the nursing side. They made a hurriedly constructed open-air operating theatre—just a frame on which to slide the stretcher cases, with mosquito netting to allow the light in. Dried blood plasma from the precious supplies had to be used, including fluid bags of saline-dextrose solution to replace fluids lost with bleeding. Anaesthetic apparatus of the most basic kind was already available at the hospital. Everything they possessed, everything they had used so reluctantly, so sparingly, had to be brought into action—instrument sets; drape packs gamma-sterilised before deployment so they could be used immediately, then cleaned and sterilised for use again by immersion in Resiguard; Betadine surgical scrub for both skin preparation and scrubbing-up. In the evening, illumination was to be provided by half a dozen small Coleman oil-lamps in order to save the already much overworked generator.

That day Louise was assisting as Piers stitched a serious stomach wound after removing several large pieces of shrapnel from the unconscious patient. He dared not probe too deeply for bullets, with no X-rays available. If any pieces remained, the best they could do was clean and stitch. Louise was far beyond feeling tired—if anything, her exhausted mind was on a high. Now she seemed able to work tirelessly on automatic pilot as she'd done for hours on end.

Piers signalled to Jan to remove the patient. 'He's the last but one of the serious group,' Piers told him. 'As I understand it, that makes four still to regain consciousness.'

'Two already have; two are vomiting, but OK.'

'Thank God!' Piers said grimly. 'Thanks also to Him we've no seriously injured children here. Do you know there's only one hospital for youngsters in the whole of Afghanistan with a general surgery facility. Consequently they get the worst cases from all over the country. The Indira Gandhi Hospital in Kabul—they do some marvellous work.'

While Piers was talking to keep himself awake, Alain appeared from the wards where he'd been attending to minor surgical repairs; all continuity of staff rotas had been reduced to the survival of the fittest. He gave them a huge smile, as if he'd been enjoying himself. 'Well,' he beamed, 'that's decreased quite a few of the cases, Piers.' He glanced at the operating table. 'You're nearly finished yourself?'

Piers gave a tired smile above his mask. 'Just one more, Alain. I was going to call you in anyway. I'd like you to take over here, if you don't mind.' He threw a glance behind him where two slightly injured men with bandaged limbs were carrying in the next stretcher-borne patient under Jan's guidance. 'What's this one, Louise?' Piers frowned. 'Louise, are you all right?'

She had swayed, looking at the hastily scribbled label on the patient's wrist. 'Yes. . .yes, I'm fine. . .um. . . er. . .' she stammered, quite suddenly hardly able to co-ordinate her thoughts. 'This one is. . .shrapnel deeply embedded in thigh, left——'

'Thanks. OK,' Piers said abruptly, his eyes fastened anxiously on Louise. 'That's it, then. Alain. Louise and I have, I think, just about had it. We've been down to danger-level and back several times.' He peeled off the disposable clothing, flinging sterile gloves aside for scrubbing and re-use. 'It's over to you, then, Alain. Louise, you're off duty as from now!'

Like an automaton she discarded her theatre-wear, hardly knowing what she was doing, while Alain blinked a slightly bemused acknowledgement to Piers.

Louise wasn't the fainting type. . .and yet she felt most peculiar. Funny how she seemed to sway towards Piers as they moved away from the theatre area. . .funny how her legs felt so feather-weight beneath her. Something was happening. . .she couldn't walk. . .the ground was rising up to meet her, and then there was only a pit of blackness into which she was falling. . .falling.

When she came to, she was convinced she was still in the theatre and tried to struggle up. But suddenly she caught the sweet fragrance of night air about her and realised she was half sitting, half lying on the ground against Piers. 'I. . . I'm sorry. What. . .happened?' Bemused, she tried to focus her eyes properly.

'Lie still, Louise,' he ordered softly. 'You went out for a second or two, that's all, and who can wonder?'

She was aware of his hand stroking back her hair, holding her with such tenderness. A small, languid sigh escaped her and she almost wished these moments would go on and on. But almost immediately her mind cleared, and she managed a smile. 'You must think I'm a softie! I've never fainted before in my life. I'm fine now, really!'

He grinned and helped her up, still keeping an arm about her. 'Let's take a stroll for a few minutes.'

Neither spoke as they walked under the stars. Both were too exhausted for pleasantries, and, briefly, Louise felt a great closeness between them with only the silence of the surrounding countryside for company. At length Piers said quietly, 'Everyone's been terrific these last few days. You in particular, Louise. The others too, of course—Jan, Monique, even Alain. He took over just now without a murmur.'

Tired as she was, Louise felt a great pang of relief that perhaps some good had come out of their efforts. 'Let's hope things will look up from now on.'

'I hope so, especially for the Muj's sake,' he said, stifling a yawn. 'It's been very bad for them. When the Commander got back to Zari he seemed devastated. I believe he's lost many men.'

Louise walked slowly, almost trance-like. 'I heard that

the last patient with the severe thigh wound is his second-in-command as well as his best friend. Is there any chance of survival?'

'Well, all I can say is that this is Alain's chance to prove himself. It certainly didn't need someone like myself, feeling as I was. . .' Piers stopped to run both hands over his eyes as if hardly able to see. 'Should the man survive, *Insh'Allah*—God willing—it'll be a while yet before he's working with Anjum again. Poor fellow, the Commander won't be too happy when we have to tell him, and that's the good news.'

They made their way back to Louise's quarters. 'Goodnight, Piers, and thank you,' she said softly.

Her face was touched by moonlight, ethereal almost, and the man at her side in his weariness felt a great tenderness for this willowy, frail-looking girl who possessed such a will of iron. He took her hand, brushing it with his lips. '*Bon soir*, Louise. Sleep well.'

For a further week their lives ran in more or less the same pattern of work until they barely knew which day it was. On one occasion, when Louise had gone to bed in her usual clapped-out state, she was startled to wakefulness by the muffled sound of crying.

It was Monique, sitting out of bed, propped up against the wall, sobbing her heart out. Swiftly Louise was at the girl's side. Monique had worked so hard to prove that she'd recovered from the miscarriage. Now she was overwrought. 'Monique, love, can I get you anything? You shouldn't be getting yourself worked up like this!'

Monique blew her nose. 'Sorry, Louise, I did not want to wake you.'

Louise squatted on the floor beside her. 'Don't be crazy, you've been doing far too much just lately.'

'*Non, non.* . .it is OK. But I 'ave to tell you something.'

'Go ahead.'

'That night you and Piers 'ad been working so 'ard,

then Alain took over——' Monique broke off suddenly, looking troubled.

'Go on, Monique.'

'They wanted my 'elp that night. I. . . I can 'ardly explain, I promised. . .' she whispered hoarsely.

Louise put a comforting arm around her. 'For heaven's sake, we're good enough friends by now for you to trust me. What is it? No, don't answer that. I'll go and see if I can rustle up some tea—you look as if you need something.'

In minutes Louise was back with two beakers which Sabia had helped provide. She rummaged in her canvas bag and found a biscuit for each of them. 'Come on, love, have this, it's much better than an aspirin with your tea!'

Monique appeared calmer now. 'This is lovely, thank you,' she murmured, sipping the tea slowly. 'Per'aps I am making a big fuss. I think maybe. . . I am over the top with everything!'

'You've been terrific! Piers said so.'

Monique smiled absently. 'Per'aps if I talk about it as 'ypothetical it will be easier. You do not mind?'

'Of course not,' Louise said quietly.

'You see, there are these three people working together, one of whom is their superior. This one 'as been stressed and suddenly snaps when confronted by what 'e 'as to do. The other two realise they must 'elp 'im, be loyal because 'e is under strain. One of the others steps in and does the job instead, while the superior manages to give instructions and talk the volunteer through it. Eventually they finish, and both assure the superior that nothing will be said of this. . .'appening. . .' Monique's eyes met Louise's, and she averted them quickly.

Louise placed a gentle hand over the other girl's. 'We *are* talking about Alain, aren't we?'

'*Oui.*' Monique's eyes filled with tears again. 'I promised I would say nothing. You see, it is like letting my country down. I am sure 'e just needs more time to readjust.'

Louise frowned. 'So it was Jan who removed the shrapnel from the patient's thigh?'

Monique nodded, lips quivering. 'Yes, 'e 'ad done more theatre work than I, and there was little time. You see, Alain's hands would not stop trembling, so 'e could not perform the operation. Eventually I did the suturing, and by this time Alain was in a very bad way, and seemed unable to get 'imself together. We just sent 'im back to 'is quarters with a sleeping pill. 'E begged us not to say anything to anyone. We promised, of course. . .but. . .' Tears choked her. 'I am worried about 'im, Louise. There is something so un'appy behind those smiles and the good nature.'

Louise thrust her hair back with her hands, her dilemma since Piers' questioning even worse now. 'Monique, I don't know what to say. It was obviously a good job you and Jan did. The man survived, and it's to your credit. But Alain. . .' Her brow crinkled anxiously. 'It's so difficult. Nevertheless, as you know Piers has softened somewhat about sending him back since all the casualties came in, and he seems to have shelved the problem.'

Monique was clearly recovering after getting the incident off her mind. She put aside the beaker. 'It could work, Louise. We could keep the whole thing from Piers.'

'We could certainly try. . .'

'It might give us time to make sure that Alain recovers sufficiently to satisfy Piers, and then per'aps this bad patch will be forgotten.'

'What does Jan think?'

''E understands. To me, 'e understands many things for one so young. Once 'e was. . .a. . .playboy—girls, parties—but now 'e 'as changed very much. 'E will not tell Piers, I know.'

Louise nodded thoughtfully. 'Well, that's a relief

anyway. But, Monique, you must get a little more sleep now. You're sure you're no longer unhappy about it all?'

Monique was already on her bed. 'Un'appy per'aps that I 'ave broken a confidence, but 'appy I 'ave taken it from my chest.' She smiled, looking more like her old self.

Later in bed, Louise asked, 'What is Anna like?'

'Very pretty, of course. The only child of rich parents. All the time I knew Jan in Paris, I 'ear that 'e tries to do big things, you know? To make 'er proud of 'im. I do not know why. 'E seems to be driven to proving 'imself to 'er. Maybe it is because 'e 'as no rich parents—no parents at all, and needs to show 'er 'is worth in other ways.'

'Do I look anything like Anna?' Louise asked drowsily.

'I do not think so. Why?'

'Oh, nothing, just something Jan said.'

Next day, despite cancelling the clinics while inundated with extra work, Piers and Louise saw some of the pregnant mothers who had queued hopefully all morning. It was decided that first-time mothers should be seen in preference. Physical examinations were made, blood and urine tests taken and blood-pressure and medical histories recorded as far as was possible. The women were instructed to attend the clinic every four weeks.

Piers, stethoscope dangling round his neck, gave a short sigh as the last patient left armed with vitamin pills. 'I'm convinced they don't understand a half of what we're trying to do.' He ran a hand round the back of his neck as if castigating himself for the situation. 'One day perhaps they will.'

'They're all fatalists,' Louise said, sticking name and date labels on to tube samples. 'I suppose you know that some of them actually have no idea how babies are conceived?'

Piers gave a worn smile of infinite sweetness. 'Yes, I do know, Louise. Being the fatalists they are too, Afghan women don't actually give their babies the breast. Their belief is that if a child in its mother's arms can't find the breast itself and they starve as a consequence, then that's Allah's will.'

'Incredible!' Louise gave Piers a quizzical look. 'Is it a fact, Piers, that you've actually specialised in obstetrics, apart from your being an orthopaedic surgeon?'

'For a while, yes. Mostly academic with very little practice. But my intention was to do as much studying as possible if I intended setting forth on these trips. Far better to have a wider knowledge of many things than to excel in one. Certainly in the Third World. That was made quite clear to me at the Médicins Sans Frontières Bureau in Paris. It's useless if we're not seen to be adaptable, inventive——' He broke off suddenly. 'Which reminds me of Alain, and——'

To Louise's great relief, at that moment Commander Anjum chose to appear, having returned from his duties elsewhere, smilingly carrying a basket of fresh fruit on each arm. He addressed them with gratitude in his eyes. 'Doctors, just a very small gift to thank you and the team for what you have done for my men.' His sensitive face softened. 'And the job you did on Moheb Khan, my friend. Your Dr Savarin saved his life, yes?' The voice held a note of challenge that made Piers answer rather guardedly.

'Indeed, Commander.'

'He is busy at the moment, I understand?'

'That is correct.' Piers smiled. 'Moheb is not off the danger list yet, but, as you know, we have high hopes for better news.'

'I may see him?'

Piers escorted the Commander to where the man lay on one of two ancient bedsteads reserved for sick patients. Moheb Khan's eyes lit up when he saw his visitor, and the two men engaged in a low, five-minute

conversation, until, at a sign from Piers, the Commander
embraced his friend and left. At the doorway, Monique
appeared with the dressing-trolley. The Commander
flashed a bright smile at her.

'Morning, Sister! It is good to see you around again!
You will take good care of my friend Moheb, I know. I
will come in again tonight.'

Monique looked slightly flustered. 'I will do my best,
Commander.' She smiled, never forgetting his kindness
to her on the night she had so nearly lost her life. When
he had gone, she and Sabia finished Moheb's dressing,
then returned to the veranda-cum-office, where Louise
was attempting to make the place look a little like its
former self.

'Hi, Monique! One good thing about working out
here—no fear of being snowed under with forms waiting
to be filled in!'

Monique's pale cheeks actually had a becoming blush
to them; she had not realised how the Commander had
noticed and appreciated it. 'Louise,' she said quickly,
'do you think now that the Commander's back 'e will
ask Alain. . .minute details of Moheb's operation?'

Louise bit her lip. 'I wish I knew. The report in the
book on that night seems adequate; we can only worry
about it when the time comes, I think.'

The time came sooner than she thought. Following a
conversation with the Commander, Piers obviously had
second thoughts about the importance of Moheb Khan's
presence, and that evening while Louise was on duty
decided to give the patient a thorough examination.
Louise remained silent at his side as Piers made small
sounds of approval on observing the cleanly sutured
wounds. 'Mmm, I can't fault Alain there,' he murmured.
'He's done a good enough job. . .'

He addressed the smiling man brightly. 'Well, Moheb,
you're progressing now. We're all very pleased.'

Almost shaking with relief, Louise went to find
Monique as soon as she could to put her mind at ease.

Later, over the evening meal, they all discussed the patients they'd been able to discharge, and those who could attend as outpatients. When they had finished eating, Jan pulled out his notebook, statistics having an endless fascination for him when he was preparing columns for his newspaper even though he had no idea when exactly they might reach his editor's desk. 'In my opinion,' he said, 'we need only keep a few in here. These Muj are a tough bunch and they can't wait to get back to their units.' He stood up suddenly. 'Which reminds me, I'm due back on the ward. Bye!'

'Which also reminds me,' Piers remarked, watching Jan hurry away, 'that I intend working out different work schedules now the heat's off, to enable us to have longer rest periods.'

'Cheers!' Alain said, lounging back in his chair.

Piers shot Alain a pained look. 'Varsha's on duty at the moment with Jan, is she, Louise?'

'Yes. Maybe I'll have time now to see what it was that upset her so much before the casualties came in. Anyone know if she's OK now?' Louise asked.

'I've seen 'er in tears several times,' Monique said, 'particularly when that giant of a man comes in—the rebel whose 'and Louise stitched, Piers, after 'e fainted— she looks as nervous as a kitten when 'e appears. It might just be coincidence, but something's getting at 'er.'

Piers smiled at Monique, his attitude warmer now since she had at no time indulged in self-pity over her private life, and her work was of the best. 'Well, if anyone can get it out of her, Monique, it's you!'

'I heard "the big one" wants to marry Varsha,' Alain observed, smiling ruefully. 'Usually it would depend on how many camels her parents could provide for her, but this man is a professional soldier and those things are no longer of first importance.'

Louise frowned. 'In that case, wouldn't it cancel out the marriage?'

'Not necessarily,' Piers joined in. 'The Afghans are a canny people, and hard cash can be just as attractive as a marriage dowry these days. There are many ways they save money—for instance, if a man's brother loses his life, he is expected to marry the bereaved woman even though he may already have one wife. They believe firmly in these things, and they do have a certain logic.'

'Perhaps. . .' Louise murmured. 'Did Varsha's parents plan this marriage, do you think—if this is the case?'

'Quite likely,' Piers said. 'Once a girl has reached puberty she's considered to be of marriageable age. The fact that Varsha's eighteen is probably giving her parents a hard time. They probably only avoid losing face with the neighbours by pointing out that most able-bodied men are away fighting for the cause.'

'It's uncivilised!' Louise exclaimed with feeling. 'Varsha wants to do her nurse's training and go away to Kabul for it, or Peshawar. She told me that when we first arrived. She'd even go over the Russian border to train. They are educating many young Afghans despite the troubles; the problem is they don't always want to return to their homeland afterwards, as we know.'

'That's the way things are. We ourselves must have no political bias whatsoever,' he spelt out.

'But surely it's part of our job to help where we can if a member of the staff's unhappy,' Louise said sharply, annoyed at Piers' attitude.

'Of course,' Piers said tersely, 'but only to a point. Remember the other rule, that neither do we get emotionally involved.' His eyes clashed with hers, and it was if he was flinging her a message that had a deeper, more meaningful significance.

Louise remained silent. Monique made an attempt to smooth ruffled feathers, but Piers stood up, running a hand across his forehead as if to ward off a pain there. 'Excuse me, I have some writing to do,' he said.

Alain left shortly afterwards, and Monique said, 'Piers was touchy tonight. It is not like 'im.'

'We can't blame him, I suppose,' Louise said. 'It's not easy trying to keep things running smoothly—or, perhaps I should say, people.'

'I think 'e's been suffering from 'eadaches lately, although 'e 'as not complained,' Monique mused. 'I admire that man, 'e is so resolute.'

Louise said nothing, but she felt again the same pang of concern for Piers. Monique was right about the headaches—she herself had noticed it.

That night Louise hoped to have a shower before bed. This consisted of standing naked on a raised mud floor and tipping a tin of tepid water over her while running the soap over her silky skin. This accomplished, she attended once again to her insect bites with antiseptic salve. Then, with Monique, she fetched two more tins of water which was used for hair-washing, the whole operation leaving them only just enough strength to get into bed!

Two evenings later Piers seemed detached, reticent, when he joined them for their meal. Louise observed that he hardly ate a thing, and, during coffee, sat leafing through a medical journal, his eyes broodily introspective. Once or twice he massaged his temple while glancing towards the doorway as if watching for Alain. When he put in an appearance, Piers still said little, and Louise wondered if he continued to harbour grave doubts about Alain's remaining with them.

Jan was just finishing his third cup of coffee, and jotting in his notebook, when he said briskly, 'Now, how would you two girls like to go to a local wrestling match here?'

Monique chuckled. 'I think so, don't you, Louise?'

'Whew! Just imagine it—the mind boggles! I've still a few spaces left in my social diary. When is it?'

'Anjum's organising it, so he'll tell us. You realise that you two females will be privileged?'

Monique threw a large piece of *nan* at Jan as he dodged out of the door and into the sultry rain that was falling.

Alain began discussing the day's cases, looking pleased. 'Thank heaven we've had no more children in with cold symptoms. The two we already have are down to normal temps now, and could be discharged tomorrow, in my opinion.'

'Have you checked for Koplik's spots inside the mouth?' Piers asked unexpectedly.

'No sign at all.'

'You're quite sure about that?' Piers sounded as if he were trying to wring a clear answer from a child, although Alain did not appear to notice it.

'Of course, Piers.'

'How long is it, Alain, since you dealt with a case of measles?'

Alain suddenly appeared flustered and hurt by the question. 'My dear chap, give me some credit for knowing what I'm talking about! Those children were admitted after their mothers reported them being fretful, with runny noses and eyes, sneezing—symptoms they've had now for ten days. I thought it worth being extra vigilant admitting them as a precautionary measure against measles. But now I think I was wrong, and a good thing too.'

'You haven't answered my question, Alain,' Piers said more pleasantly. 'In Paris you are a working surgeon, not a general practitioner. In no way am I criticising you or your diagnosis, but the fact remains that it's very easy to lose touch with details of certain childish ailments, as I'm sure you'd agree.'

Alain smiled fixedly. 'Naturally, but I didn't come away without bringing a couple of up-to-date textbooks with me.'

'I'm sure we've all done that. Forgive me if I appear to be questioning your word—believe me, it was purely concern for you as a colleague, apart from trying to

prevent any sort of medical complications.' Charm
flowed from Piers' voice, sincerity from his smile; all
giving Alain the reassurance he so badly needed.

Yet Louise felt she was witnessing the gradual demo-
lition of Alain's weak armour.

'No offence taken, Piers,' Alain replied good-
humouredly. 'I'm with you absolutely. We must try and
head anything off that's likely to eat into our medical
supplies.'

Piers' eyes beneath the lids had been watchful, as if
waiting for Alain to fall neatly into the hole he'd prepared
for him. 'Indeed. To get back to these Koplik's spots—
if they're missed. You mentioned that the young
patients' temps had returned to normal. Again, this can
be deceptive. You may find tomorrow that this opinion
is finally refuted and the rash has actually shown itself.
If you recall, it starts after ten to fourteen days, behind
the ears,' he said brusquely. 'This needs spelling out,
because epidemics mean disaster for us here, particularly
at this stage.' He glanced at the two girls, who seemed
to have been sitting without drawing breath. 'Would you
both agree that checking and re-checking is vital on
something that could create havoc here of major
proportions?'

Monique and Louise readily murmured their assent.
Monique anxiously dwelling on whether Piers was using
this argument to cover his true anxiety for Alain's
capability as a surgeon.

Yet still Alain appeared lulled into a sense of false
security with his superior, as he smiled benignly. 'You're
absolutely right, of course, Piers.'

Louise was feeling more and more uncomfortable, and
sensed that Piers was acting like Kara Kush, biding his
time before the final swoop on his prey. He was quite
correct in being circumspect. She sipped her coffee,
trying to keep her eyes from meeting Monique's. Her
friend was tense when Alain's integrity was under scrutiny, and that fact alone highlighted just how tenuous

Alain's position was if something were to go wrong now after all their efforts to help him. She tried to change the subject.

'The wrestling match Jan mentioned—have *you* any idea, Piers, where it might be held?'

Piers seemed not to have heard her; he looked exhausted, and beneath the tan was a grey pallor which she had not noticed before. Her words seemed to reach him suddenly. 'The wrestling match? Somewhere— um—on the other side of the valley, I believe. No doubt the Commander has to be sure it's held in a safe place. I imagine he can put his mind to that now that Moheb is showing such an improvement, for which,' he smiled, rising from the table, 'we have Alain to thank. Incidentally, Alain, I'd be happier if Monique and yourself would go to the ward now to make another check on those children. Varsha's on duty, and she'll give you the latest on them. Meanwhile,' he turned to Louise, 'we'll go and look out those vaccine cartons just in case they're needed in a hurry. Perhaps you'd give me a hand.'

Since the fire, the store-room had been less useful than before, but fortunately the medical supplies were still reasonably safe on high shelves. Piers handed Louise a torch. 'I think there's still something left in the batteries! Direct it this way while I'm hauling the cartons out, would you, please?'

Moonlight filtered into the shadowy area, and the damp, pungent atmosphere and suffocating humidity were unpleasant as she watched Piers stretch up to the shelf he wanted, his back muscles moving strongly beneath the shirt he wore, his shoulders wide, his hips narrower than when they had first arrived here.

He took down the large carton, and as he did so a smaller wooden box flew from where it had been concealed on top of the carton and came hurtling towards him. He stepped swiftly in front of Louise to protect her, and the box caught him a heavy blow on the forehead, causing him to stagger back, blood gushing from the deep gash.' 'Damn and blast!' he cursed as he held a handkerchief over it.

Louise wrested the carton from him. 'Oh, lord, Piers!' she cried. 'We'll go straight to the ward and see to it immediately. . .'

'Don't fuss, Louise, it's all right.' But he followed her just the same. As it transpired, she needed to put two stitches in the wound, and managed to pack him off to bed with a sleeping pill. What she didn't tell him was that the offending box had contained heroin, and that in the heat of the moment she had rammed it into her pocket.

Next morning Piers did not put in an appearance. Louise reached his quarters just as he was leaving to go on duty. As she was about to remonstrate with him, he seemed to stagger, and was soaked with perspiration, words issuing from his lips making no sense at all.

Her heart missed several beats as she tried to stop him falling, but he keeled over to the ground in what appeared to be a terrible spasm of uncontrollable shuddering.

CHAPTER NINE

LOUISE called for help, and between them Jan, Monique and herself got Piers on to a stretcher, then transferred him to one of the two bedsteads behind the curtained area.

With a damp cloth Louise sponged Piers' face. His dark eyes fluttered open, the awesome trembling of the lean, powerful body arrested briefly. His parched lips moved. 'Malaria. . .quinine tablets. . .my room. . .'

She sent Jan rushing for them, and Monique for fresh pillows, as well as a bowl of cold water for head compresses. By the time she had the tablets, and had crushed them into drinking-water, Piers seemed to have drifted away already.

Louise and Monique between them raised him up, putting the cup to his lips. 'Drink, Piers, drink!' Louise urged desperately. He just managed it before the fever overtook him ferociously, bathing him in sweat. Gently they lowered him back on to the pillows. Monique looked worried.

'Can you care for 'im on your own, Louise? I will come to 'elp you as soon as I can.'

'It's OK, Monique, don't worry. You go.'

Don't worry, Louise almost sobbed to herself as she was left alone with Piers. A bout of malaria like this could take hours or even days before it swept its way through the victim. She just had to reduce the fever to bring down the raging temperature that racked him. As she removed the soaking-wet garments he wore, tears blinded her eyes as he lay like a gentle Goliath, weak as a kitten, and giving only an occasional moan as she towelled his body dry—it would remain so for mere seconds. A low, incoherent mutter burst from him. His

134

fine head tossed from side to side in torment, every part of him fighting this parasite that had attacked him.

Monique came back later with a few fresh, cool white sheets, one of which Louise spread over Piers in place of an old curtain. Louise thanked the girl and carried on applying cold compresses to his forehead. The black-brown eyes had fluttered open momentarily, then closed just as quickly. 'Everything's fine, Piers,' she whispered, knowing he wouldn't hear. 'Don't worry about anything.' She was talking for its own sake. With the rest of the staff having to stick to their usual duties, she knew there were hours ahead yet of watching over him not knowing the outcome, but she would not leave him.

Through the night, one of the staff took over while she snatched a couple of hours' sleep out of sheer exhaustion, insisting on remaining there in case of any change.

By dawn next day the treatment was automatic. Louise would sponge him down yet again with fresh, cool water, dry him off, and quite suddenly his hand would grip hers as if to reassure her, then just as suddenly his hold would become as frail as a baby's. For seventy-two hours she stayed at her bedside vigil, her eyes hollow with lack of sleep, worry permanently nagging now as to the possibility of getting him back to Peshawar to hospital.

Another dawn glimmered through the open doorway of the ward. She was too bone-weary to do any more than lie stretched out at the side of Piers' bed until he stirred. When he did at that moment, she rubbed her eyes with balled fists, flexed her shoulders and straightened her back. The air seemed a little cooler and birds were singing. She checked Piers with the usual apprehension, wondering how much longer he could carry on in this weakened state. But, to her great joy and delight, a wan smile flickered across his face, and his eyes opened, free of the burning, feverish light she had come to expect.

'Louise,' he muttered, gripping her hand, his eyes

closing before he miraculously slipped into a normal sleep that was health-giving and tranquil.

'He's through it,' said Alain an hour later. 'No need for hospital now.' They watched as he lay sleeping naturally, brow no longer soaked in perspiration, nor the handsome features contorted with pain. His breathing was regular, his skin cool, and, almost as if in concern for them, he'd roused himself sufficiently to indicate that the worst was over before falling asleep again.

'Come along, my dear,' Alain was saying with great solicitude. 'We'll take care of him now. You must get to bed at once, otherwise you'll be in trouble.'

Monique saw Louise to her room, fussing over her, making certain she had all she wanted before sleep overtook her. She had heard Piers whisper her name, and knew now that she could succumb to the rest she craved. Refreshed in mind and body, she slept for a full twenty-four hours.

The next time she saw Piers he was being told in no uncertain terms by Sabia that he had to stay put until she would allow him up. Feeling a brand-new person herself, Louise smiled when she saw him sitting up dutifully in bed, brown torso in such contrast to the white sheet. He was very much in Sabia's capable hands. 'He is far better, Dr Holden,' Sabia said officiously. 'I tell the doctor he must rest now.'

'You're quite right, Sabia.' Louise smiled, her eyes sparkling. 'I think between us all we'll manage it!' When Sabia had left them, Louise sat on the side of his bed. 'Great to see you in the land of the living once more!'

He grinned, his tanned, strong face glowing now with no longer any sign of malarial pallor. 'I always believe in having the best medics around me!'

'How long have you had malaria?'

'Several years now. Ever since I worked in the tropics. I have frequent medical check-ups to keep an eye on it, but I'm assured that so long as I've always got quinine I'm OK. Luckily it's only a mild strain by now, but those nasty little bugs have a habit of turning up at the most inhospitable times. I imagine things have been getting me down recently. That bang on the head must have been the symbolic end to my trying to fight it! Time I had those stitches out, I suppose.'

Later Louise performed the small job, at the same time remembering the box and its contents still in the pocket of her dress where she'd thrust it when everything but Piers had been blocked from her mind. Even so, she would not trouble him by handing it over at this stage. He needed as much rest as they could insist upon.

He'd been watching her as she worked, and, when she pushed the trolley away behind the curtain, he said quietly, 'Each time I seemed about to fall into a dark, bottomless pit, you were there.' He took her hand, gentling it as if it was something special. 'Thank you, Louise. . .' His eyes held hers, the dark recesses holding far more than she could comprehend.

Colour rushed to her face. 'It's marvellous to see you fit again,' she said, hoping her feelings towards him were not obvious. 'Everyone's knuckled down to keeping things going, and we're all agreed that it's staying that way until you're really a hundred per cent.' They talked on for a while, then she slipped her hand from his, standing suddenly, not wanting him to have the merest idea how chaotic her thoughts had become. It was as if she'd been overwhelmed by a tidal wave of feeling for him that had mentally flattened her. It was deep, exalted, almost noble, far removed from any physical inference, yet it struck her with unreasoning fear. Her subconscious desire never to love again surfaced, bringing with it the repercussions of loneliness, despair and rejection.

Swiftly she regained her outward professional cool. 'Alain and I think you should have at least a further twenty-four hours' complete rest, Piers, so I'll leave you to sleep now, and in another week you'll be much fitter than we are!'

For the rest of that day her thoughts bound her. She

hardly communicated with the others, so engrossed was she in the shock revelation of her feelings for Piers Morell; the total impracticability of it; even worse, the weakness of her own complete reversal after the way Raymond had treated her. Her implacable avowal of resistance to ever again fall in love had been completely swept from under her. All she could do now was to conclude that their present claustrophobic existence was partly to blame, and she simply had to put the entire thing from her mind.

In two days' time no one could prevent Piers from getting back on duty again. He was holding an antenatal clinic that day, conducting a carefully worded question-and-answer session with a pregnant woman, when Varsha came rushing in. Louise was standing by to assist the patient with the least necessary movement of the dark, voluminous robes she wore, in order that Piers could examine her without violating all her traditional beliefs.

'Dr Holden, please come! It's the children!'

Louise left the clinic as soon as she decently could, Piers' mouth set in a thin line when he'd heard Varsha's excitable demand.

On the ward, Louise and Varsha were looking at the two children, Varsha opening her own mouth and pointing inside, then doing the same to the children. Louise gave a loud groan. She checked inside the young mouths and the dreaded spots were there for all to see. Varsha was looking pleased with herself, and Louise knew she was waiting to be praised. 'You have done well, Varsha. How did you know about these spots?'

The girl nodded, smiling, measuring one hand to the size of a toddler, and another taller. 'Sister. . .and brother,' she murmured shyly.

'I see, yes.'

Louise waited for the explosion when she told Piers the news.

'You mean to say that Savarin missed it after all?' he

erupted. His patient looked at him anxiously, and quickly he gave her a reassuring smile and helped her from the examination table, telling her to come again in four weeks' time. Once they were alone, he sagged against the table. 'Good God, I just don't believe it!'

Louise was already defending Alain without realising it. 'Well, quite obviously it hadn't shown itself until tonight.'

He rounded on her, thumping the table with his fist. 'Louise! Why are you constantly carrying the can for Alain Savarin? Why is it that every time there's a discussion about him you're there to support him?' He thrust both hands in his trouser pockets as if distrusting them. 'I just don't understand! Surely you realise how necessary it is to keep people on their toes in a set-up like this? You of all people, who's had such an excellent training in London, should know there's no room for shilly-shallying in medicine, particularly in such a climate. For God's sake, woman,' he flung out his hands imploringly, 'how do you expect me to feel when I seem to have no positive back-up from you? Come to think of it, even Monique goes all patriotic when we discuss the man. What sort of people have I got around me? I feel I can no longer trust my own judgement!'

Louise knew he was right, but for the wrong reasons. Her pity for Alain had widened into a protective attitude for Piers too, to prevent him from having all the extra hassle and anxiety of sending Alain back, and thereafter waiting maybe three months minus a male doctor in their team. Yet, as she looked at Piers' scowling countenance, she was almost compelled to give him the real reason, for her own anger was rising at the way he'd rounded on her—but she desisted. Instead she said coolly, 'You cannot prevent people from drawing their own conclusions, Piers.'

'No one is disputing that! But tell me, how can I keep this team going, delegating responsibility and all it entails, if one of us is going to continuously break the rules?'

'I wouldn't put it as strongly as that. Alain does what he thinks is right and——'

'Balderdash!' he roared, cutting off her sentence. 'He knows as well as I do he's not pulling his weight, and I for one will not tolerate it! OK, I appreciate everything that's been done for me while I was sick; you all kept the clinic going, and I'm grateful to you for that. And yet doesn't it seem strange to you that the minute I'm on the scene again one of Alain's. . .erroneous blunders turns up? Why doesn't he come clean and tell me he's not up to the job? Maybe he has trouble back home—I don't know. I can't make head nor tail of the man. . .' He gave her a discerning glance suddenly. 'Unless. . .'

'Unless what, Piers?'

'Yes,' he was pondering, 'why the hell didn't I think of it before?'

'Piers, for heaven's sake, what are you trying to say?'

He swung away from the table, taking a stride towards her. 'That you and Alain are. . .are more than interested in each other, hence the cover-up from you! After all, you've had ample opportunity for this to happen. Some of those occasions when he's been on night duty and you're on call? Very romantic! What's to stop you being "on call" to him whenever the inclination presents itself?'

The words stung Louise like a whip, lashing her sensitivity, striking at her heart. She fought not to let herself down, not to let him see how much this accusation had wounded her. A mountain cave in the flickering flames of firelight had turned to grey ashes in her mouth. The new brilliance of the admiration she felt for Piers, too fragile lest its beauty be marred, was now rapidly dying a death.

She gave a harsh laugh. 'That's the best joke I've heard since we've been here, Piers. Have you got any more like that?'

He jerked her to him suddenly, his hands gripping her

shoulders and almost shaking her in his fury. 'Sarcasm doesn't become you! Can't you see that I must leave no stone unturned in order to explain Alain's machinations to myself? What I said to you just then no doubt should have been put differently, with more finesse, diplomacy, you may think, but what the hell does it matter so long as this problem is resolved? All I want from you is a straight yes or no to my line of questioning. I don't want vague answers laced with acrimony. I put the question to you again, Louise: is there anything at all between yourself and Alain?'

She took a deep breath to steady her voice, having felt a slight trembling of his hands as they dropped from her. He was not fit enough yet for all this aggression. 'No, Piers,' she said wanly, 'there is not.'

A slight pause hovered between them like a living thing, as if the brevity of her reply had nonplussed him. He ran his fingers through his hair. 'Very well,' he said briskly, 'I'll now go and see the children for myself. I'd like you to be there too.'

In the children's section, set slightly apart, lay the two victims, both with heightened temperatures. Piers studied the chart Louise handed him. 'Yes,' he sighed, 'it seems to be taking the usual pattern, I'm afraid.' He ruffled the eight-year-old girl's hair with a smile, and told her to open her mouth. The examination revealed an eruption of tiny white spots. 'Like grains of salt on a slightly reddened base. . .' he quoted almost to himself, before discarding the spatula and washing his hands, then moving to the next child. He was a three-year-old boy, flushed and fretful, and not so willing to allow Piers to examine him. Louise steadied the child's head. Piers talked quietly to the boy, pacifying him as he calmed down. 'Not so easy to see with this young man,' Piers murmured. 'Ah, here we are, inside the cheeks by the molars—our old friend, the Koplik's spots. Another three to four days and a macular rash will develop. . .' He looked at Louise, who was by now trying to make the little boy as comfortable as possible. 'We'll start the treatment with aspirin, Louise,' he said, 'to help bring the fever down—oh, yes, and soothing lotion of some kind for the skin. Keeping the children isolated is the problem. But you know the rest, and don't forget, keep the light from the eyes as much as possible.'

They left the children in Varsha's care, Piers saying to Louise, 'We'll see what sort of check we can get from old records, such as they are, on those who've been immunised and those who haven't. Starting with the children here in the clinic queue with their mothers. Excluding those who are pregnant, of course.'

It took two weeks, devoting most of that time to the immunisation of children, particularly those of around nine months old. They seemed to swarm from everywhere with their mothers once it was known that the treatment would prevent a highly infectious disease among them and their families. The village women listened painstakingly to Louise and Monique, promising to bring into the clinic anyone who showed sign or symptom of measles. Again, the entire team worked tirelessly to prevent the scourge sweeping the village, and gradually, by a slow and watchful process of elimination, they appeared to contain it. Tension lessened and the expected epidemic appeared to recede.

A few days later Louise was in the store, searching a cupboard to see if there was a precious carton of vaccine they might have overlooked in case another scare developed, when her disappointment at not finding one was overtaken by surprise at seeing yet another small box exactly the same as the one she'd found before and done nothing about during Piers' bout of malaria. This time, checking what it contained—a quantity of heroin as before—she knew it was far too coincidental for it not to be suspicious. Someone was using the clinic to pass the drug along in a chain of sale, of that she was certain.

She went in search of Piers. The animosity between them had faded since the night he'd accused her about

Alain. The measles emergency had taken up their every waking moment. It was early afternoon and blisteringly hot when Louise went into the common-room, where she found Piers writing up the endless reports that had to be attended to and sent to Paris whenever any of the Commander's men were moving out to Peshawar. Any really important post was handled this way, Jan too managing to get his dispatches moving by the same method.

Piers looked up from where he sat on the colourful cushions against whitewashed walls. It was comparatively cool, and he seemed surrounded by a sea of papers. 'Louise?' he queried.

'I think we have a slight problem—but,' she said, seeing the unlined brow suddenly draw together, 'it seems to be just diplomacy and tact that's needed.' She reminded him of how she had found the first box.

'Oh, no!' he groaned. 'What happened to it?'

'Nothing. I was concerned about you and put it aside, thinking we'd discuss it with the Commander, then came your malaria, and it was forgotten. Now I've just found a second one in the same place concealed in the store-room.'

Piers took it from her, giving a low whistle. 'Phew! You're right, Louise,' he said, confirming the contents in the box. 'I'll pass it on to the Commander and see what he suggests. Thanks for your help on this.'

Two evenings later there was time at last for them all to have a convivial meal together, and leave their work behind for a short spell. A warm, languid breeze lifted the tree branches above them, and a clear blue sky with hardly a fleck of cloud stretched away forever. Conversation had been desultory, mostly shop, over coffee, and Jan sat dreamily strumming his guitar, the sweet, melancholy notes a fitting background, which but for the mountains could have been an English summer garden.

But the tranquillity was short-lived. The sound of a

jeep suddenly shattered the peace, and arriving in a cloud of dust Commander Anjum leapt nimbly out and strode over to where they were sitting, his military appearance as impeccable as ever.

'Commander!' Piers welcomed him. 'A cup of coffee perhaps? Do join us.'

A smile lit his face as he sat between Monique and Piers. 'Many thanks! It would be delightful—you people are very kind to me. And so, how is Moheb?'

Monique, who at Anjum's express wish had made herself responsible for nursing the man, smiled confidently. 'I think you will be pleased when you see 'im tonight, Commander.'

Anjum's piercing eyes, enhanced by dark, sleek brows, and a neat, thick moustache above his beard, smiled gratefully into her eyes. 'That is good, very good. You are no longer worried about him now, I think?'

Piers looked across at Alain. 'It was your job, Alain. Over to you!'

Louise felt her toes curl with nervousness; Monique's face blanched as Alain's expression worked slightly while he found difficulty in forming his words. 'I—um— we. . .' Completely taken off his guard, he looked round in near desperation for Jan, who had earlier excused himself to write a letter. Alain cleared his throat. 'We are well satisfied, Commander. I. . .we are not anticipating any setbacks now that he is moving around a little more each day. You will begin to see quite a difference, I think.'

Anjum's eyes had not left Alain's face as he spoke. 'Yes, I understand, Doctor. Excellent. . .excellent.' He glanced at Piers warmly. 'I am sure that Mr Morell would have no objection if I brought any other casualties of this kind specifically to you, Dr Savarin. Moheb has great faith in your work.'

Alain, who appeared to have shrunk back within himself in the last few seconds, now re-emerged, a smile illuminating his round, rather shiny face—with relief, no doubt, rather than acceptance of praise. 'Thank you, Commander, you do me a great honour.'

To Louise the words were grovelling, and yet to Alain, who throughout his entire life had hardly pleased anyone, she supposed they were probably wrung from him in sincerity even though laden with guilt.

The embarrassing moment seemed to end abruptly with fresh coffee for the Commander, and conversation swinging back and forth between them all. Anjum, who was in animated repartee with Monique about Paris, glanced at his watch a short time later. 'Forgive me, I must visit Moheb, and then attend a meeting with my aides.' He sighed wistfully. 'We all miss Moheb very much, but if he had died,' he threw up his hands, looking at Monique, 'how *terrible*!'

Alain by now looked tired and pale beneath his tan. He stood up. 'If you'll excuse me, I think I'll go and take a look at some of our young patients.'

Piers broke off from his reading suddenly. 'Alain, I've not yet had the chance to apologise to you for blaming you for the measles break-out. I hope you'll forget it, it wasn't really your fault. With these people it's difficult to know if they understand our questions even if they say they do. The whole thing could have fizzled out as a common cold, as you said at the time, or it could have been that the incubating period had not quite run itself out—hence no symptoms for us to diagnose. Anyhow,' he smiled disarmingly, 'luck was with us after all. No ill feelings, I hope?'

For the second time that evening, Alain looked flustered, but pleased. 'None at all, Piers, and. . .thank you.'

That night in bed, Louise told Monique about the incident. 'I'm sure Piers would never have apologised to Alain had he known it was Jan who performed on Moheb. Provided Moheb recovers sufficiently, Monique, it looks as if we should agree once and for all to keep this to ourselves for Alain's sake.'

'Quite definitely,' Monique agreed, filing her nails. 'I think I 'ave prayed each night that it be so.' She concentrated for a second, then remarked suddenly, 'Commander Anjum is a very perceptive person, do you not think, Louise?'

Louise looked at the attractive, dark-haired girl sitting cross-legged on her sleeping-bag, keeping her eyes on what she was doing, perhaps not wishing anyone to see an expression of pleasure there. 'Yes, Monique, Anjum is a very fine man.'

High summer was already taking its toll with the team at Zari. Always so much work to be done, and always for a never-ending stream of lovable people who deeply appreciated everything that was done for them. Yet monotonous food, lack of sleep and constant tension were wearing down their basic good health. Feeling like grease-spots that evening, Piers and Louise wandered along the bank of the river not far from the clinic to where further upstream it tumbled into a far more spectacular waterfall. They knew each other so well by now that neither spoke as they rambled alongside the water, which was bubbling fresh and clear over the stones, making its own music.

Ever since the time Piers had accused Louise about Alain and herself, and despite his apology, she had found it best to withdraw more and more inside herself. Despite all that had happened, she still retained her unshakeable admiration for his work, his reliability and strength of purpose. And it was that which she kept in the forefront of her mind when tempers frayed. But at this moment they seemed completely at ease together, relaxed and at one with the world in such an idyllic spot.

'Hey, what a magnificent place!' said Piers, looking around him. 'I've never been this far before!' His fresh shirt and slacks gave him almost the look of a tourist without a worry in sight.

Louise smiled. 'Jan showed me weeks ago, but it's far better now.'

They reached the shining lake, which at this time of year appeared to be a huge diamond set in lush, thick dark green foliage. A waterfall higher and narrower than the one nearer the clinic, like a gleaming, ruffled grey ribbon, foamed and frothed down from the towering rocks above. Spray caught in the setting sun formed a shimmering rainbow arcing down gracefully to the dancing water.

'What an invitation for a swim,' Louise murmured, unable to take her eyes from such beauty.

'Why not?' Piers laughed, already moving from her.

'Beat you to it!' Louise challenged impulsively, darting behind a rock to cast off her scanty clothing, and she waded in before diving like a sleek porpoise. When she rose up, shiny droplets covered her—hair, spiky eyelashes and beautiful shoulders and breasts. She blinked water away from her eyes, and saw Piers already swimming strongly beneath the rainbow.

'Over here!' He beckoned. 'It's fabulous!'

She swam through the deep water towards him, her hair floating out behind her, her body smoothly elegant.

'You look like a mermaid.' He grinned, broad chest and shoulders tanned and powerful as he trod water, head thrown back, white teeth gleaming with laughter as he waited for her—carefree laughter displaying yet another glimpse of the real person, someone free from the cares he had taken upon those broad shoulders which were at times a near impossible burden.

He stretched out his hands to catch her, grasping her arms firmly, and drawing her beneath the rainbow rain, leaving them shrieking with delight like two runaways. Then for a while Louise cut loose and drifted slowly, gracefully, on her back, gazing up at the perfect sky that was free of cloud or strife.

A pair of bronzed shoulders suddenly rose up beside her. Piers' handsome face was full of devilment as he grabbed her waist playfully, his hands suddenly in contact with her velvet skin making their eyes meet. Louise caught her breath, and the blood pounded against her ribs. He looked down at the pale, distorted view of her body, the reflection enticing. . .then dived away suddenly, leaving her bereft of the dreams that had suddenly welled inside her, but which she had so soon to quell.

He was back at her side, the teasing laughter there again. 'How does one catch a mermaid?' He grinned, a sudden gush of water between them sweeping her towards him, so that for a world-stopping moment she experienced the sensuous brush of his slippery skin against hers.

She splashed him suddenly. 'Mermaids won't allow themselves to be caught!' She lunged forward with a laugh before he could interpret the thoughts in her eyes. 'Race you back!'

He won, of course. With one powerful stroke to three of hers, he was on the bank, laughing and disappearing like a shadow between the rocks. Louise dressed hurriedly, feeling refreshed and invigorated. They sat together away from the rush of the water, and watched the moon gradually grace the evening above the rim of the mountains. Louise lazed back on her elbows, Piers sitting, one leg drawn up, resting his elbow on it as he gazed rather solemnly ahead. 'There's something I have to say, Louise, in confidence.'

Her heart skipped a beat. The serious note in his voice was not the harbinger of good news. 'Yes?'

'The Commander had a word with me before he left this evening. It seems there's a strong possibility that we shall be leaving Zari sooner than we think. The rebel troops need to move on, there are fewer people now left in the village. I believe they're trying to set up larger clinic facilities that would embrace several villages over a large area, particularly to deal with casualties that continue to arrive in strategic places, and they know we just can't do what we'd like to for them.'

Louise stared at him, feeling as if the ground had suddenly opened up in front of her. As if all the plans she'd vaguely formed in her mind for the future were rushing at her far too soon, casting her back into the limbo she'd been fighting to banish. 'I. . . I don't know what to say, Piers. It's. . .it's so unforeseen.'

'It may not happen just yet. But I thought at least I should mention it—but not yet to the others.' He tugged at a tuft of grass. 'There's such a strong bond between us all, it's quite a shock to think of its ever being broken. I've never felt this way before, despite the ups and downs we've had.' His eyes were across the river, his expression withdrawn, as if already his thoughts were occupied with plans that no longer included them. 'But we must wait and see.'

CHAPTER TEN

LOUISE was on her weekly night duty the evening she returned from the swim with Piers. She was allowed to sleep, and quite often was not called upon by the staff; nevertheless, her presence near the wards was required.

In the barren silence of the night she drifted into sleep eventually, but first her mind had been spinning with the unbelievable news that Piers had given her. It had seemed almost impossible to imagine that she might soon be part of Western civilisation again, with running hot water, motor cars, fast food and television. To her they had seemed so irrelevant that she had sunk her head into her arms to try and shut out the realities.

Piers too had had little sleep. He had tried to catch up with a backlog of written work and had stayed in the common-room long after everyone else had settled down for the night. By three a.m. he flung down his pen, rubbed his eyes and made himself a cup of coffee-coloured water. Food supplies were running low again, the intake of extra patients making it a constant anxiety. He pushed the cup aside, standing and flexing his muscles, wide awake, knowing that he wouldn't sleep if he went to bed. The swim with Louise in the lake seemed in a sense to have revitalised his whole body, his mental powers, his physical, but he tried to put the thought of her from his mind.

It was very rarely that he allowed himself the luxury of dwelling on his own life and whether it was going the way he wanted. Until now it had, he supposed. He had everything a man could wish for—good health, riches, more than he needed, recognition in his profession, status wherever he went. . .and yet more than ever lately he found himself thinking of love, friendship, loyalty.

Was it possible to find such attributes in one woman?
His marriage in his youth had disproved it, and for years
he had not been prepared to share his life ever again.

Yet, if he were honest, he would admit that Louise
Holden intrigued as well as annoyed him. There were so
many things about her he didn't know, but those he did
astonished him—her resilience and strength of character,
the work she did, the way she tackled things, sometimes
under appalling conditions. She was never averse to
telling him what she thought. Her grey-green eyes would
flash and anger would spill over, followed more often
than not by a burst of humour that kept them all sane.
Her spirit seemed indomitable. Yet what—and the
thought had worried him more than ever lately—if her
liaison with Alain Savarin was serious? She denied it, he
knew, but there were things he couldn't help noticing:
her gentleness when she spoke to Alain, the near adora-
tion on his face when he looked at her, the long
conversations they enjoyed. But in Piers' opinion they
were hopelessly wrong for each other.

He shrugged, trying to cast off the thoughts as he
strolled outside into the soft, overwhelming beauty of
the night. Why should he concern himself with Louise
and her personal life? Soon, according to the
Commander, things were about to change. The team
would return to Paris, and a chapter in all their lives
would be ended. He stopped walking suddenly, hearing
the desolate call of a nightbird, the distant bark of a dog,
the rustle of grass as a nocturnal creature moved effort-
lessly in the shadows, and overall, the musky smell of
lush vegetation cooling after a day's intense heat.

Louise tossed and turned in her sleep, her brain far too
active for the sleep she needed. Fragmented scenes of
the wedding crossed her vision. . .sheer exhaustion
brought its own uninvited result. . .

Raymond was pointing at her, so too was the girl with
him: the laughing crowd scoffed as her wedding gown

fell from her, leaving her naked and at the mercy of the screaming taunts.

'No! Leave me alone. . . I hate you, do you understand?'

Raymond came closer. . .closer. . . Haunted, Louise thrust her hands out before her, pushing him. 'No! No!' her terrified screams rang out.

Piers strolled towards the clinic, his thoughts still roaming. At this time of night it gave one the chance to ponder on things. Even the night calls of animals had a certain rightness. Then came another cry, not an animal this time. . .but surely a child? A woman? There it was again. Swiftly he remembered Louise was on call sleeping in the clinic. He broke into a run. Anyone could have got into the place. . .

'Raymond!' It was Louise. 'Go away! I hate you. . . I hate you!' She was sitting up, arms flailing wildly, eyes closed, screaming, her face contorted with panic.

'My God—Louise!' Piers dropped to the mattress, taking her gently into his arms waving away the young auxiliary who had rushed to the scene. Louise's arms were pushing him from her, her strength incredible as she fought to resist him. Tears of anguish poured down her face. At last he managed to hold her to him, murmuring her name.

'Louise. . .Louise. . .' He stroked her hair, his arms firmly steadying her trembling body against his chest. 'My dear, it's Piers. Don't upset yourself. . . Please, what's this all about? I can't bear to see you this way. . .'

Her ragged breathing gradually levelled. Tear-washed emerald eyes stared wide at him as she pushed her hair from her face, unable to reconcile her thoughts. Her whole body was shaking with the frenzied madness of the nightmare that had claimed her after weeks, months of thinking she was free of it. Piers comforted her, gentling her face, waiting for her to recover, calling for a glass of water to be brought, while he held and soothed her.

The auxiliary hastened to do his bidding, her brown eyes full of pity for the Miss Doctor who worked so hard.

Piers held the cup to Louise's trembling lips, her teeth chattering on its edge before she was able to drink. At last came a wan smile of recognition. 'Thanks, Piers. Sorry about making such a fuss. . .bad nightmare, I'm afraid.' Her head had flopped on to his broad shoulder. She felt like a rag doll, but in a minute or so she managed to move from him a little, lest he thought she was unable to overcome such childish things as nightmares.

'I'll tell the nurse you're going back to your own room for another couple of hours' decent sleep,' he told her, deep compassion in his voice. 'I'll take over for you.'

She did not demur; her mind was still in a daze of clashing emotions which seemed to drain all her energy and resistance.

In her room, Monique lay sleeping, a quiet, rhythmic, ladylike snore confirming it. Piers smiled. 'If you're sure you're OK now,' he whispered to Louise 'I suggest you take a mild sleeping pill, and I'll see you in the morning.'

A few hours later, Monique gave a little smile when she saw Louise beside her just before they got up. 'I do not blame you for knocking a few hours off your night duty! I would do it if I 'ad your strength of will!'

Louise grinned. 'Nothing so laudable, Monique! It was one of my wretched nightmares. And who do you think had to hear all the commotion? Yes, Piers Morell, who else?'

Monique rolled her eyes upwards. '*Mon Dieu*! What did 'e say? I am glad it was not me! Just lately 'e seems so 'igh and mighty again!'

'He was all right really—sent me back here and told me to take a sleeping pill. It seems he couldn't have been sleeping himself. Just my bad luck, I suppose.' Louise attempted to be as casual as she could.

''E will not 'old it against you! Why should 'e? Sometimes I wonder about that man. After working with 'im, I love 'im a leetle, and 'ate 'im a leetle.'

Louise yawned and got up. 'That just about sums it up for me too, Monique!'

Piers said nothing further to Louise about her troublesome night. She thought he was slightly more considerate to her for a few hours or so, until a sudden influx of outpatients, snaking away from the clinic and endlessly into the sunset, it seemed, concentrated their minds for the rest of the day. Another week went by in this way, as if the local villagers were trying desperately to make up for the times when other more serious casualties came in to take their place.

It was on a particularly brilliant morning under a silver-blue sky that their spirits rose considerably. In the valley, water ran fast and clear between banks of blue-white daisies. Distant fields of ripening wheat and maize lay neatly terraced between high stone walls. Apricots hung ripening on the trees, and they had only to shake those around the clinic and down came the fruit in a shower of golden rain.

Commander Anjum chose that morning also to visit the few remaining of his wounded men, but it was Moheb Khan, soon to be discharged, who troubled him.

When he came into the office after seeing his friend, the Commander was obviously worried. 'It is not like Moheb—I do not understand. His wounds have healed, but something else is troubling him, I know it.' A smile lit his face. 'That man is like my brother. We know he must pull himself together, but he seems unable to do this. Whatever it is, we must find out. Mr Morell tells me he can find nothing else wrong, Dr Savarin the same.' He thrust his hands out in an ardent appeal. 'What must I do to help him?'

Monique, who often seemed to possess the ability to say the right thing to Anjum without receiving one of his occasionally fiery looks, said quietly, 'It may 'ave nothing to do with 'is wound, Commander. Per'aps the man 'as trouble in 'is family. A wife, maybe; many children. . .' Monique's lower lip curled down in her inimitable style.

The Commander's astute eyes softened. 'Yes, you may be right. My thoughts have little time for such things. His wife died, but he has a child who is looked after by his sister-in-law. Perhaps there is gossip, I do not know.'

It seemed Monique had got it right again. 'Then I think you must talk with 'im. It could be that 'e likes 'is wife's sister, but 'as been away very much. If, as we understand, tradition 'ere expects that 'e marries 'is sister-in-law, then the poor woman is un'appy because Moheb does not want to discuss, some would say, unimportant things with 'er because 'is Commander 'as many other very big things on 'is mind. . .'

Anjum was nodding thoughtfully in agreement, a light of comprehension dawning in his eyes. 'Of course. . .yes, indeed!' The animated face sparkled with laughter suddenly. 'I think there is something wrong with me too, hey? Usually it is I who cares for the welfare of my men, and today, Monique, I am seeking advice from you!'

Monique's dark eyes teased his. 'It is nothing, Commander. We all need 'elp at times!'

Louise, who had finished the drugs round of patients, went to the cupboard to replace the fast-diminishing stocks and lock them away. Monique and Anjum were doing a good job for *entente cordiale* without her standing in on their conversation, she thought with a quiet grin, as neither noticed her slip away.

Outside, the noonday heat struck like a shaft of flame. Piers had just left the wards, and, when at length he'd accompanied the Commander to his jeep, he joined her and they walked towards the blessed shade of the trees. They flung themselves down on the grass, grateful for the lunch break, even though it was only apricots and *nan* for the fifth day running. 'Before the others join us, Louise, about that heroin. At last the Commander's taking action. As you know, he was extremely put out when I told him about it. Now he intends asking a few of his trusted men to keep their ears open. He didn't want to do it, apparently, but nothing's been forthcoming. At the same time he asks for permission for another man to spend all night concealed in the store-room from now on until we see who is involved. It might still have to be a process of slow elimination, but he's determined to get to the bottom of it, seeing that the clinic's been drawn in.'

Jan suddenly appeared, flinging himself into the easy pose they'd all acquired when sitting on the hard ground. 'Wow! Some heat!'

Piers grinned. 'Hi, Jan. Like to see the menu?'

Jan laughed. 'I'd like to see a cold beer!'

'Don't torture yourself, my lad,' Louise teased. 'Although, come to think of it, so would I.' She lay backed suddenly, gazing up at the trees. 'Hey, what about making some apricot wine? Just imagine that, all the lovely cold golden liquid trickling slowly down our parched throats!'

Piers and Jan pounced on her playfully, picking her up amid her shrieks and threatening to toss her into the air a hundred times. 'Or,' Piers said gleefully, 'the alternative will be tying you to a tree while I spell out some of my favourite mouthwatering recipes from home, and the minute the rest of us see you drool, you'll be tortured by tickling!' As they lowered her to terra firma, promising never to mention such a thing again, with much laughter, Alain and Monique arrived and joined them for lunch.

'Hey, girls, whatever happened to that wrestling match we were going to, remember?' asked Jan, squelching into an apricot.

'I think the Commander has more important things on his mind just now,' Louise said wryly, indicating the man himself being driven away by the 'Big One', who seemed to be his new factotum.

'I don't think much of that great hulking guy,' Jan said suddenly. 'There's something about him that gets my back up.'

'He's a coward, we know that, don't we, Alain?' Louise grinned, not realising the way Piers had observed the closeness between them. 'He only has to take a look at a syringe and he faints!'

That night, when darkness fell, one of Anjum's men was settled into the store-room by Piers. He came back on to the ward, where Louise had just finished dressing a shrapnel wound, looking quite pleased with himself. At the wash bowl he said to Louise, 'If anyone finds the culprit that man will! I shouldn't like to be on the other end of his fists!' He was still grinning at the thought when they did a round of bed patients together. And at long last an element of peace and healing on the ward could be sensed. Maybe just for a short time, but it was a good feeling. For once, too, they had no children as in-patients, which was also a step in the right direction.

As they crossed the compound to go to their rooms before the evening meal, Piers asked, 'No more night-mares lately, I hope?'

'Fortunately not,' Louise said casually. 'I imagine it was one of those strange happenings that might never occur again in a lifetime!' she fibbed.

Piers gave her a sideways glance. He had his own ideas about that. 'I just hope you're right!'

'No problem!' she said jokily. In fact, since the last nightmare, it was fighting back and then finding herself in Piers' arms that was the thing she couldn't forget; his murmured assurances, the urgent concern in his voice. Despite everything she still could not wholly abandon the intensity of feeling that had overcome her on the day he had recovered from his malaria. Whatever excuses she found, even when he was in one of his sarcastically cutting moods, the knowledge of that deeply held affinity for him free of all other constraints would not be denied.

With nothing revealed as yet concerning the heroin, Commander Anjum called again two days later to see the man on surveillance. He also spent a few minutes with Moheb, which to anyone noticing such things was a good enough reason to call regularly at the clinic, although he was still much concerned with affairs of his beloved country.

Louise and Jan, with Monique, were having a mid-morning drink under the trees talking in a desultory fashion about clinic affairs when Jan said suddenly, 'Incidentally, Louise, Monique told me that you know I did Moheb's op instead of Alain. What a night!' He grinned. 'Monique and I went through agonies wondering whether to say anything or not; but in the end I'm glad she did, seeing that we still have to be cautious!'

Louise nodded. 'You did a terrific job, Jan. Alain should be eternally grateful to you.'

'In his funny way I think he is. I'd like to think someone would help *me* out of a hole if I needed it.' Jan stared across absently at the Commander's vehicle. 'Alain was speaking to me the other morning, saying how glad he was that you didn't know,' he said wryly. 'I think he's very keen that you see him in a good light, Louise!'

'Well, I'll never let on if he doesn't. I just hope the whole thing fades now.' Louise finished drinking her goat's milk, shuddering because it was slightly sour. 'Look, isn't that the Big One nipping out of the jeep to waylay our little Varsha?'

To their amazement they witnessed the huge man intercept Varsha as she crossed to the kitchen. Conversation became heated and they moved out of view, then sounds of aggression were heard and a female scream broke out.

Louise jumped up. 'That's Varsha! My God, why didn't we take more notice when the poor girl was upset recently?' She and Jan ran to the kitchen, just in time to see the Big One raise a burly hand and knock Varsha heavily to the ground.

Jan immediately piled in, taking a flying leap at the bully and felling him, and the two then looked set to perform their own wrestling match as they battled on the ground with immense agility until it seemed one was intent on murdering the other. Louise and Monique's cries to desist went unheeded, but the noise brought Commander Anjum to the scene. His face was a hard mask of fury as he hurled a stream of abuse at the rebel, pulling him off Jan, who had blood streaming from his cheek and was nursing an injured arm.

In seconds the Commander's vehicle had shot away in a cloud of dust. Hearing the commotion, Alain and Piers arrived, too late, and everyone began talking at once. Jan was brushing himself down, dabbing his face with the cloth Louise had given him.

'What the devil's going on?' asked Piers, as Jan staggered slightly, shirt in tatters and an ugly bruise forming on his wrist.

'I'm OK, thanks, Piers. Fine, in fact! I did not intend standing by and watching that big palooka harm Varsha—she's been unhappy enough as it is lately. By the way, where is she?

The girl had obviously vanished during the fray, it had all happened so quickly. Louise shaded her eyes from the sun, scanning the landscape.

'Not a sign. The poor girl has probably gone home in a fright, and who can blame her?'

Piers looked concerned. 'Take one of the horses, Alain, would you,' he instructed. 'She can't be far away, and I'll get Jan fixed up.'

Monique was frowning. 'The trouble must 'ave some bearing on the tears we 'ave seen. That bully 'ad something to do with it.'

Louise and Piers glanced at each other with swift understanding. Were they getting the first clue about the concealed heroin at last?

'It may not be anything too much, Monique,' Piers said. 'These people are very excitable, as we know.'

At the back of Louise's mind she recalled Piers' angry remonstrance to her over not getting emotionally involved with the locals. This could be just a private tiff and nothing as serious as drug concealment, but, even so, the problem had to be cleared up.

They had not realised as they returned to the ward that some of the convalescent patients, including Moheb, had witnessed the unpleasant scene while sitting against a wall in the sun. It had caused a great buzz of excitement, and Louise would not have been surprised if they had been gambling on the outcome! Nevertheless, gossip would spread, no doubt to the village and beyond, Louise concluded, as they prepared for an afternoon outdoor clinic. An hour later Alain returned alone.

'She's in her home, but would not budge, neither would she say a word. Her mother's not much help— she keeps yelling at her like a fishwife. As I left, the only thing I could get from Varsha was that she wants to speak to Louise or Monique,' Alain said as he dismounted.

Monique, who was due to assist Alain with some minor surgery that afternoon, said, 'I think Louise should go. We 'ave a string of patients waiting for us. Is that OK with you, Louise?'

'Sure. Can you spare me, Piers?' she asked, as he listened to the exchange.

'Yes. I think I'd better come too in case there's any trouble. We'll take the horses. From the latest info I'm told vehicles, petrol and arms are very valuable commodities just now.'

It was a warm, clear day, above them the sky was a cloudless blue, and, riding beside Piers over the bridge which spanned the limpid, shining water, Louise felt a sudden rush of joy. The neat fields about them were planted with potato and root crops, the maize plants halfway up the side of the valley were tall and green, and strewn all round were more stones and rocks than she would have ever imagined possible in such mountainous country.

Piers seemed to sense her thoughts. 'For a place so inhospitable, it's a near miracle what they manage to do.'

She stifled a sigh. 'Is there any more news on whether we leave here shortly or not?'

'Nothing yet, no. I haven't seen Anjum since he went off in such a temper over the scuffle with his driver and Jan. Incidentally, I don't want to say much to Varsha until we know more.' He gave Louise an admonishing look as the horses clip-clopped along together over the rough ground. 'Sentiment must be curbed, Louise, and not a word about drugs. We'll leave that to the Commander if and when our suspicion is confirmed.'

She did not answer. For one thing, it was necessary to guide her horse carefully over the loose stones, and for another, she felt the stirrings of resentment at his high-handed tone. 'Piers, do you mind? I'm not a child! It may have escaped your notice that I'm twenty-six years old, and well able to work out a thing or two for myself!' She tossed her head angrily, her back ramrod-straight, slim, capable hands gripping the reins tightly as she urged her horse forward.

Piers did the same, catching up with her, a supercilious smile on his features. 'On such dangerous terrain, Louise, you continue to show childish traits, which goes to prove that what I said earlier is quite correct!'

Still smarting, but determined to ignore the remark, she straightened her shoulders and concentrated her mind on Varsha and her troubles as they rode into the village. After a brief enquiry they found the mud and wood house where Varsha lived with her mother, sisters and brothers. They were invited inside immediately. A woman sat in a corner wearing the usual robes, a veil extending across her face with a mesh-like panel through which to see. She busied herself weaving coloured wools on a hand-worked loom until Varsha joined them. The

girl's arms were full of freshly cooked *nan* straight from
the oven, which she offered them with mugs of tea and
dishes of raisins. She introduced the woman as her
mother. The woman inclined her head, remaining silent
throughout, contrary to Alain's report, but appearing to
understand the conversation that ensued.

'My mother, she is very angry,' Varsha told them.
Piers nodded, talking to the girl in Farsi; Louise, silent
now, was seated on a cushion on the floor.

When the rest of the discussion changed to English,
Piers said to Louise, 'Varsha's mother expects her to
marry Abdul Gul, the Big One. He's willing to take her
even though she's no longer young, according to him.
Thirty-eight himself, he's willing to take a chance with
her. When he's away as one of Anjum's crack guerrilla
fighters banging off rockets and artillery fire, he wants
to know he has a wife and a home to come back to.'

Impassively Varsha listened, then she said, 'I will not
marry him. I want to work in hospital.'

Louise knew Piers was expecting her to choose her
words with care. 'Could you not marry as Abdul wishes,
and still work with us?'

The girl shook her head. 'Abdul Gul will not allow
this.'

Piers frowned. 'Maybe if I speak to Abdul——' but
the girl was already reacting fiercely.

'No. I shall kill myself,' she said, her huge eyes hard
suddenly.

Louise glanced at the mother, who was still deeply
engrossed in her work and yet occasionally her hard
bright eyes understood. 'You must not talk that way,
Varsha,' Louise said. 'Come back to work tomorrow and
we will see what can be done.' She hardly knew what the
options were in a situation of this kind, but it was the
best she could think of. She gave the girl a sympathetic
smile. 'We'll see you in the morning, then.'

They extracted a promise to that effect before leaving,
then both she and Piers remained silent with their own

thoughts until they were well away from the village. They stopped on the bank of the river, allowing their mounts to drink, and tethered them in the shade, leaving them to crop contentedly. 'Let's hang on for a while,' Piers said, gazing up at the cloudless sky. 'There may not be many more chances.'

They walked through patches of root crops, up a side valley, the maize field at the top bright with poppies. Louise gasped at the drifts of wild lavender covering the dun hillside, the pale purple flowers in great profusion. She crushed some between her fingers—they were deliciously fragrant, although less strong than English lavender. Skirting an old bomb crater, they passed the corner of the maize field to a meadow on the lower slopes that was full of bluish-mauve clover, the scent almost overpowering, the river singing in the sunshine below.

Louise dropped to the ground, sliding the peasant scarf from her hair and running her fingers through it with a sigh of bliss. 'This is marvellous, Piers!' she called, flinging herself back amid the pungent flowers and grasses.

Piers laughed, joining her. 'You're right, why shouldn't we snatch a few stolen moments?'

Louise lay looking up at the sky, nibbling a long stalk of grass. 'You know, all the ugliness in the world is wiped out in moments like these.'

Piers chuckled, turning to smile at her tanned, animated face and the rosy colour beneath, as she peered up at the sun, green eyes sparkling enough to put the bright river to shame. 'You're a romantic,' he told her, at the same time wondering why he had never before noticed a delightful tiny mole at the base of her neck. 'And not only that. . .'

'Yes?' Louise grinned, their eyes meeting as if preparing to clash.

'You *are* still a child.' He drew a finger across her brow, smoothed a wisp of hair from her cheek. 'And before you start breathing fire and brimstone at me again,' his firm mouth was above hers as he laughed, 'I love it. You have all the wide-eyed wonder of a child, the appreciation of the world around you, and——' he moved slightly, allowing the full length of his virile body to rest against hers '—and at times, the innocence.'

His lips skimmed hers, teased like the flutter of a moth's wing, then grazed over the fine contours of her face, returning to her waiting lips, kissing them in a firm contact which was lacking in any sexual urgency.

Louise sensed it meant. . .goodbye? There was a finality about it, a holding back that in such perfect surroundings would not, could not have happened with any normally red-blooded man.

He was smiling down at her, then he kissed the tip of her nose. 'Shall I tell you something?'

She nodded, unable to speak, for the surge of indisputable knowledge was there again—the deep affinity, the glow of her admiration for him—and that day, lying in the heady fragrance of the clover-drenched meadow, there was more, incredible as it seemed. Was it love? She could hardly look into his eyes for fear he read the sheer magnitude of her thoughts there, and the desolation already waiting.

Piers' smile was teasing. 'This moment will stay with me always. Wherever I am in the world I shall only have to be near a field of clover, to smell its fragrance, and you'll be there!' He sat up suddenly, pulling her with him, carefully removing a full-petalled clover caught in the shining tresses of her hair.

With an effort she gave a low-pitched laugh. 'I really appreciate that thought, Piers!' But for her the day had lost its brightness, the sky its blue.

They sauntered back to where the horses waited in the shadow of a rock, Piers untethering both and handing over her reins. His face was thoughtful as he stood with his back to the animal, one arm leaning on the creature's flank. 'Seeing that we must come down to earth, Louise,' he said with a wry smile, 'we'd better return to matters in hand. I still think we've no right to interfere with the ways of these people. Varsha and Abdul whatever-his-name-is will have to fight it out between them. If on the other hand there's any suggestion of drug dealing, then that's an entirely different matter. But we don't know that yet, do we?'

'I see no reason why the girl can't sleep at the hospital if she's being pestered by this man. OK, it's purely. . .tribal, if you like. He wants to marry Varsha and she doesn't want to. Surely we can help her do what *she* chooses in this day and age?'

'That's rather a simplification, if I may say so,' Piers retorted curtly. 'There are other considerations. It would only take Abdul and couple of his beefy henchmen to tear the hospital apart if they had a mind to. I still don't think you realise how tempers flare in these countries. I've seen it happen many times, over far less than choosing a bride! I know how you feel, but ultimately it's up to us to respect their rules and traditions.'

Louise shrugged her shoulders suddenly with a defeatist air. 'Very well, Piers, I'll go along with you on that, whatever my personal thoughts, but quite honestly I don't think we've heard the last of this business. Abdul's probably got it in for Jan now anyway!'

'Exactly! He'll have to curb his knight errant act. How do we know Abdul isn't convinced that Jan has *his* eyes on Varsha?' Piers said sharply. 'I think we've enough hassle at the moment without starting up another war of our own!'

Her brief moment of capitulation was shortlived. 'For heaven's sake, Piers,' she burst out, 'in the last few seconds you've exaggerated things out of all proportion! Varsha isn't a fool. She wants to be a qualified nurse, to start her training in Kabul, perhaps. If she's old enough to get married, she's old enough to leave her mother and decide on her own life! Many other young women are doing this in the cities here—it's only in the isolated rural areas where they cling to the old ways!' Her green eyes flashed in the sun, her stubborn chin thrust out as she confronted Piers with her equally determined ideas, and which neither would forgo.

'I still say they must work it out for themselves!'

'I'm amazed at that, coming from you! I thought you'd have been the first to encourage these girls to escape from the old bondage!' she hurled at him, not caring about the smouldering disapproval in his eyes.

He took a step and caught her suddenly by the arms. 'Louise, for God's sake stop trying to do more out here than was intended. Stick to your medical work! In a few months' time you'll be back on the other side of the world, and by then there'll no doubt be hundreds of other Varshas fighting at their own pace for what they want. So can we just forget it for now, and concentrate upon what's expected of us?'

She tightened her lips, mounting the horse, and glanced at Piers as he leapt on to his—so haughty, so irritating. . .so stubborn! 'Just one more thing, Piers,' she said icily. 'All I'm asking is that we try and give Varsha a reason for living instead of contemplating suicide!'

He did not answer, neither was he talkative on the way home. All she could think of was that she had marred what had been a near perfect afternoon. . .and it would never come again.

CHAPTER ELEVEN

JUST before sunset, when the light was wonderfully pure and gentle and the whole landscape hushed, Piers and Louise arrived back at the clinic. From across the valley the high, clear voice of the Mullah's call to prayer rang out on the calm evening air.

The evening meal was delayed somewhat while they reported what had happened at Varsha's home, the account being left to Piers to edit as he thought fit. Louise noticed that he still held no brief for either Varsha or Abdul Gul and their problems, which continued to irritate her.

Monique was looking relieved. 'Thank 'eaven, you 'ave at least got 'er to come back 'ere. Varsha is a good worker,' she shrugged, 'but whether she loves 'im or leaves 'im, it cannot be our concern.'

Louise did not think that her friend's summing-up was the right one either. But perhaps time would tell.

Two further weeks passed and nothing yet had come to light about the heroin. The security man was still with them, but even he was getting impatient with the inactivity, despite there being a rota of three.

Varsha had returned to the clinic, and Abdul Gul had not been seen since the Commander had removed him on the day of the fight. They had admitted another spate of more serious Mujaheddin casualties, who had all needed surgery. This had been apart from one poor woman who had travelled for four days on horseback with a retained placenta and in a very bad state until Piers and Louise had put it right with curettage. At length the work-load eased off and they could actually contemplate eating together once again, which on this particular evening was just as well, for it turned out to be one of those occasions not easy to forget.

They had just started their meal in the common-room, out of reach of most insects, when one of the auxiliaries appeared, wishing to speak to the doctor. By that, everyone meant Piers Morell. He went off with the girl, leaving the rest of them to speculate what could be so urgent. But Piers was back long before their sharp wit could think of anything.

He looked stern, and said quickly, 'Louise, I want to see you out here!' Which, once they were alone, immediately set tongues wagging and jokes circulating—anything to take their minds off the boiled goat and rice!

Outside, Piers said seriously, 'Louise, I want you to come across to the office, seeing that you were the one who found the heroin.'

Louise glanced at him quickly. 'Developments?'

'Yes,' he said as they entered the office, 'and here's the offender!'

Standing beside the security man was Varsha—no tears, no submissive, downtrodden air about her, only a defiant scowl on her face. She paused only briefly in the middle of a stream of curses as they came in. The boxes of heroin were on the table in front of her and, with a little help from the security man, she had admitted to concealing them, and was promptly removed unceremoniously to the village, where the Commander would be waiting for her.

Their meal forgotten, the team still could not believe that quiet, gentle Varsha had turned into the criminal virago she really was. Piers shook his head. 'Heaven only knows what the full story is, but no doubt the Commander will tell us.

And when the Commander arrived next day there was no pretence about seeing Moheb in order to cover his presence there. 'Some of the women are far worse than the men at this game,' he told them. 'Varsha was able to acquire the drug from different patients who turned up here—more often than not wounded men making money by acting as couriers as they moved around. Varsha was one, but she was also in charge of a wider operation and selling the stuff to the Russians, using the clinic as a go-between. She had no intention of doing her formal nurse's training as such; she was biding her time by putting on an act, particularly with the last team of medics, who were really taken in by her, as you were!'

'What about Abdul Gul?' asked Louise.

'He knew nothing of her dealings and only wanted her for his woman. She was stringing him along in order to gain your pity and attention, which would put you off her real game. Her acting abilities stood her in good stead.' Commander Anjum shook his head. 'She will be dealt with by the appropriate authorities, and I will hand these boxes over also. Now I must go. Later I must meet several other Commanders for an important conference between us.' He glanced at Piers, the feverish light of patriotism burning in his eyes. 'There may be something to tell you later, Mr Morell. Meanwhile, thank you all again for your help.'

Louise watched him go. 'It seems you were right all along, Piers, about getting involved,' she said quietly. 'I'll learn.'

Piers smiled. 'We all have to eventually.'

Later, Alain was taking a clinic with Louise, who was telling him how she'd been so completely taken in by Varsha, particularly when they had visited her home. 'I'd have staked my next dinner on her being OK!' she protested, screwing on the top of a Savlon jar. 'Though, come to think of it, all that *nan* and tea and raisins must have proved something!'

Alain grinned, looking far happier now that Moheb was ready to be discharged, the wounds healed to his satisfaction. Piers apparently still did not know about the terrible occasion when he had had to hand over to Jan. Now he smiled back at Louise, thinking how wonderfully attractive she looked in her Muslim dress. 'Ah, well, it just goes to show; never trust a woman!'

A week later the Commander called to tell them that the clinic was to be closed down, and from then on turned into a first-aid post and store for medical supplies. A group of reliable people from the village would be in charge of it. 'My men and I will be moving to Kabul, Doctor. There is much to be done and my presence is needed there. But do not worry, I shall arrange that you be accompanied by another unit on its way to Peshawar also. You will be looked after as before. Any unfit patients still in your care will be transferred and taken care of. I am sad; everyone is sad.' His eyes looked over-bright, then he added with a wide smile and an optimistic note, 'Never mind! We will celebrate our undying friendship together when the day comes. Also, Moheb will be marrying his sister-in-law, and we shall have a big party altogether, hey?'

Even Piers was bemused by the suddenness of it all, though he had been warned. No doubt the meeting of the Commanders had put the final stamp on their decision. The Mujaheddin were carrying on the fight for what they believed to be their cause. Had it been the opposing Government troops with whom they'd spent so long, Piers knew that both he and the team would be just as overwhelmed by the wrench of parting.

It was to be at least another two weeks before final arrangements were completed for the departure from Zari. The team, on the night of Commander Anjum's news, were dumbstruck when Piers told them. It seemed to take days for the news to sink in, followed by a morose contemplation of the place that had now turned into a little Eden before their eyes. Individually they all had private thoughts to rearrange in their minds as well as their problems. They sat talking whenever they were together.

Jan shook his head. 'We've all learned a great deal

from these people, yet it's such a wild and backward country. . .'

Monique nodded agreement. 'In our different ways we each 'ave something to be thankful for.'

The heart-searching continued deep into the night without every thought being voiced. Monique had gone through the trauma of losing her baby and the man she'd loved. She was stronger now in mind and body, renewed and heartened at what she had overcome, and soon would be seeing her beloved Paris once more and making a fresh start.

Jan on first hearing the news had wanted to withdraw within himself. His thoughts reeled at the possibility of taking up his married life with his Anna. He seemed unable to believe there was a chance of seeing her again. Unless she'd grown tired of waiting for him—was there someone else. . .? He'd matured since coming to Zari, he knew that, but would things be the same?

Alain was cautiously optimistic in his pondering. Provided his secret remained with his friends, he would return to Paris and divorce Hélène, of this he was absolutely certain. He would then spend the rest of his life working in the Third World after a period of further medical training to fit him for such work. The dream he cherished was that one day perhaps Louise might want to see him again. That was where he had to switch off his thoughts. He could only return home full of hope.

Piers as yet could think of little more than the hazardous journey back and his responsibilities as such. If he did allow himself to dwell upon his life in Paris at all, it would be to stay in his penthouse apartment for a short time attending to business affairs. After visiting his parents in Scotland, he would then consider the offers he'd had to continue his work in other parts of the globe. In fact, his personal life seemed to be just a vast, barren waste. He knew in his heart that the only female—the only friend—he really felt at ease with was Louise

Holden. When it came to no longer seeing her each day his enthusiasm for life would be sorely diminished.

Louise, who had carried the burden of her silent misery throughout the trip except for a brief mention of it to Monique, knew that it had gradually, almost unwittingly fallen from her. She had gone through a long black tunnel and emerged whole at the other end. Her recent nightmare had been brought on, she was sure, by complete exhaustion, and seemed to have been obliterated entirely since she had woken up to Piers' comforting presence. He supplied all the loving sympathy and reassurance she had so desperately longed for at the time of the jilting but would allow no one, not even her parents, to give. It was a battle she had had to fight alone, and, in the suppression of it, her tortured mind had exploded into those distressingly horrifying nightmares which she had at first convinced herself were a form of guilt on her part. For the solace Piers had given her, she would be ever grateful. She wondered if they would meet from time to time, or would they all so quickly be absorbed back into their respective lives and forget?

The clinic was now emptied of patients, the medical supplies, meagre as they were, were locked in cupboards, and plans went ahead for entertaining the three hundred or so people who would be attending the grand party.

On the appointed day, excitement rose, and, after snatching a few hours' extra sleep that morning, Louise and Monique showered, and dressed in their best Muslim gowns, which they had bought from a village woman who was an excellent seamstress. Louise wore one almost the exact colour of her eyes, the emerald cotton soft as silk, and Monique's was the same in cream, complementing her dark colouring.

By sunset, when the wedding of Moheb and Roshana was due to take place following the call to prayer, all males and females gathered together again on the cool green grass in the small garden in readiness for the marriage. Roshana, a beautiful girl of twenty, her slender ankles and wrists weighed down with jewels beneath her purple and gold gown, her magnificent brown eyes heavily outlined with kohl, her sparkling and intelligent features showing through her veil, made a radiant bride. Moheb, her groom, was splendidly arrayed in a long silk cloak of rainbow stripes, a handsome turban adorning his head and happiness obvious in his animation.

The short, solemn ceremony was conducted by the Mullah, and afterwards great applause broke out, guns were fired and bonfires lit. The Commander was very much in charge of the whole affair. Gifts of money were thrown from all directions to the happy couple, music being provided by simple combinations of flute, reed and drums. Dancing followed after they had all done justice to the groaning food boards set out inside the clinic rooms, no one enquiring as to how the food came to be there in such quantity. Increasing the tempo of the celebrations by the minute with potent drinks, the party went on until dawn. Piers and Louise were taught traditional dances and songs, Monique doing everything the Commander told her, Alain and Jan making a fine couple, with laughter and tears flowing with the sheer exuberance of the occasion.

Neither politics nor wars were mentioned, and, as a fiery sun split the morning sky, most were eating final refreshments, taking at least another two hours or so before the guests began to depart. Farewells and tears flowed in equal measure for an event no one wanted to end.

Piers and Louise managed to have one last walk along the river-bank in that mother-of-pearl dawn.

'Just one more glimpse of the waterfall where we swam,' said Piers. 'We just have to see it again.'

They wandered along in the clear light, feasting their eyes on the frothing water still gleaming like a million diamonds as it fell. There was an aura of magic about it. Piers took her in his arms, their lips met, and Louise tried to bank down the fires that were rising within her. Perhaps she was glad when Piers murmured, as he drew away,

'Just one last special goodbye kiss for a souvenir, Louise.' His dark eyes smiled down into hers. 'Who knows where any of us will be a month from now? And, before I forget, you look absolutely stunning in that dress, do you know that?'

She smiled, although it hurt to do so. 'Piers, you're a great morale-booster. Just remind me of this occasion when we're on the return trip, dusty, hungry and bad-tempered, and I'm stuck at the top of a mountain pass on horseback scared silly to come down, will you?'

He threw back his head and roared with laughter. 'Louise, I don't believe you're really scared of anything now. I just thank my lucky stars I made that decision in Peshawar to have you join us.'

She shivered suddenly, and his arm tightened about her. She could hear the strong beat of his heart as his lips brushed the top of her head. 'We're all going to miss each other very much,' she murmured absently.

'Come along now, you need a few hours' sleep before we set out on the long trek home. Time enough for such talk when we actually get there!'

They left two nights later with the next caravan, a new unit of Mujahedin; another Commander in charge, horses, donkeys, mules, and personal belongings all moved out before the early autumn snow began to coat the mountain peaks. The three-week journey held much the same unknown hazards as last time. They travelled by night and slept by day. They ate only enough to keep them alive and rolled themselves into their *pattus* as resistance to cold nights and protection from the heat of the sun.

By the second week the teams talked as little as possible, all of them more debilitated than on the outward trip, all suffering from dysentery from time to time, yet still tending the medical needs of the men who travelled with them. The camaraderie between them all was quickly established, and occasionally some of the rebels would entertain them when the day was ending and they were high in the mountains. There was singing, a wrestling match, and even a competition for weight-lifting with lumps of rock!

When they reached the first of the safe houses, Monique and Louise were well looked after, with hot water for showers, and a clean mattress to sleep on. The food they had was hot, delicious soup, then some sort of mutton, followed by apples and cups of hot, sweet milk tea and fresh bread—a feast indeed.

Towards the end of the trek, approaching the border, the caravan leader sensed that something was wrong. He and Piers made the decision that both girls should sit up behind one of the magnificent horsemen. Holding their breath and clinging together, they galloped full tilt down the mountainside and over into Pakistan, never quite knowing what the emergency was! Once again they passed through the remaining checkpoints in a truck, under the guise of an ambulance, Louise prepared to treat Monique as a childbirth emergency if necessary—but it was not, to their great relief. Back in Peshawar they stayed in the same hotel for rest and treatment, unable to relax, all somehow left in limbo. Part of them was longing to return to civilisation, the other half dreading it.

Paris welcomed them back with some of its lovely, balmy September days, dawn mists lingering over the Seine, and at dusk a red sun like an over-ripe peach drifting above the trees.

Monique and Louise, after two weeks, were lazing idly in Monique's spacious apartment in Neuilly, an expensive residential area, Monique insisting they had a whole month's holiday together there until Louise decided whether or not to rent another flat in Paris.

They had spent the day at the Louvre, and had basked in the sunshine of the Tuileries Gardens, spent lavishly on ice-creams they'd only dreamed of recently, then had walked to the Place de la Concorde until their feet had cried out for home.

Louise had been less talkative than usual as they had relaxed that evening, and Monique had sensed that it had something to do with Piers Morell, although she hadn't said. Now Louise had introduced the subject of the dinner invitation again.

'Monique, what do you think I should do? Accept Piers' idea that we meet to talk about a job for me before he goes abroad again? Quite honestly, I could just as easily make a phone call to say that I prefer to make my own way.'

'Yes, but you 'ave told me 'ow it is difficult to get jobs in Britain,' Monique reminded her.

'I know; even so, it's a problem I must handle myself.' Louise tucked her bare feet beneath her on the large brocade divan in Monique's salon, giving her a wide smile. 'Oh, I'm sorry, Monique, you must be getting fed up with the subject. At least we had our reunion party last week, which was terrific. I can't forget your cooking—it's out of this world; the others were bowled over with it!'

Monique beamed with pleasure. 'I shall make it an annual event if possible, because we were all very 'appy together.'

Louise gave her friend a long look from beneath her lashes. 'Do you ever think of Commander Anjum, as I do, Monique? He was so strong, so reliable, so——'

Monique seemed unable to hold the word back. 'So. . .charming, yes?'

'Right.' Louise smiled. 'I wonder if we shall ever see him again.'

Monique's round eyes were suddenly far away, as she shrugged nonchalantly. ''Ow do we know? Life is very strange, and still 'olds all the cards for us.'

Louise nodded. 'True. Well, at least we know our friends are taking up their jobs again, and now you're starting at the American hospital near the apartment here—it sounds great!'

'I 'ope,' Monique said soulfully, although her mind seemed to be on other things.

That night, in the unbelievable comfort and luxury of her bedroom, Louise made up her mind that she would see Piers, if only to tell him that she was sorry not to be able to take up his offer regarding a job. Deep down, also, she had the feeling it might be the last time they met. For some days now she had wondered about working abroad permanently.

Three nights later she took a cab to the Place Vendome. It seemed more in keeping when dining at the Ritz, although she would have preferred riding on the Metro. Piers had sounded pleased when she'd told him she would meet him. 'In that case, we'll spoil ourselves a little!' he had told her.

She and Monique had gone to a boutique on the Boulevard St Germain, and Louise had bought an exquisitely simple soft white crêpe dress that seemed to slip on like a glove, highlighting her good points and playing down her bad.

Now, as she paid the driver off, and saw Piers, so suave and immaculate, so distinguished-looking, her anxieties about the dress completely disappeared.

'Louise!' He bent down to brush her cheek, then took her hands in his. 'You look wonderful!'

In the restaurant, although talking animatedly, neither wanted to draw too much attention from the fantastic food and wine Piers had ordered, and which had been approved by their waiter. It was an education for Louise, who had been to only the more modest hotels with her parents. Her contemporaries were always too short of cash for such luxurious living.

As dusk fell they sat in the fragrant bower of the

courtyard garden, sipping champagne, Louise casting off the sense of nervousness she'd felt on seeing the real Piers Morell that evening, the man of the world she really knew him to be.

His eyes went over her admiringly—the honey-gold breasts just showing above the low-cut neckline of her dress, the fair hair piled on top of her head, giving her sophistication with an air of quiet beauty also. He quickly switched his thoughts, saying with a smile, 'Have you had any further ideas about the job?' He noticed the sudden defensiveness in the green eyes he knew so well.

Louise fingered the emerald brooch given her by her parents on her twenty-first birthday. 'I haven't quite made up my mind yet, Piers. I'll be going home to Cornwall the week after next for a while. I might be able to work a few things out more clearly then. Please don't think I'm not grateful for your offer.'

'But what's the problem?' A small frown had appeared on his forehead. 'We can wait until you come back. I'm not without a few contacts in Paris or London, where I could make it easier for you.'

'That's not the point, Piers. I'm not certain yet *where* I want to work.'

He leaned across the bowl of autumn roses on the round table between them, touching her playfully on the chin. 'Is there something I ought to know? You were always hesitant, as I'm sure you'll remember when you first joined us. You're getting married, is that it? Perhaps now that you're back here your mind has been made up?'

The question seemed to hang in the soft air between them. Louise tried to breathe deeply to steady her voice, running her fingers over the long stem of her glass, wanting to put into words what had really happened and that Piers' supposition was quite wrong. The long-concealed feeling of inadequacy, that it was something lacking in herself that had caused the break-up—the humiliation of it still seemed to thwart all her good intentions as she murmured the hated words. 'Yes, I was going to be married about eighteen months ago now, but. . . I. . . I was jilted.' Before he could answer, it was as if a dam had burst in her mind. She told him all about Raymond; the nightmares, and how for so long it had been her burden of guilt. 'I think I'm free of it all now,' she told him quietly, 'free of all the bitterness, and most of the hurt pride.' She smiled. 'Zari has done a great deal for me in that respect. . .'

She trailed off, conscious of the deeply penetrating gaze of Piers' eyes, the dark obsidian wells a combination of surprise and compassion.

'I never dreamed,' he murmured beneath his breath. 'I have to confess that Monique mentioned the nightmares to me, but only because she was worried about you. When I witnessed it for myself, I imagined it to be a kind of stress you were going through because of the job.' He smiled suddenly, his strong, slender hand covering hers. 'Do you know, Louise, you never cease to amaze me! Until now I haven't had a chance to tell you how marvellously I thought you coped with everything at Zari. Frankly, I don't know how I'd have managed without you. *Now* you tell me you had this additional weight on your mind.' His eyes softened as he looked at her. 'I'm really sorry about it. Seems we've both had our dreams shattered, one way or the other. I can understand why you wanted to work your own way through the shock you suffered. You're such an independent, stubborn, free-spirited individual. I realise now too why you've spurned my help. Well, so be it, if that's your preference—you must do what you think is right.'

Conversation between them seemed somewhat easier then, talk invariably turning to Zari, and, when at last he took her back in a cab to Neuilly, Louise was saddened at the thought of parting. At her front door, Piers momentarily held her hand in his, pressing it to his lips while smiling at her with his eyes so that she almost cried out in her need to escape, in case she made an utter fool of herself. 'I must go, Piers, and thank you for a wonderful evening.'

She could not interpret the look he gave her, or the way he suddenly braced his shoulders, saying with businesslike brevity, 'I've given you the name of my club in Paris. You can always reach me there should you change your mind. Have a good holiday with your parents. *Au revoir*, Louise.'

'*Au revoir*, Piers.' She smiled, as they touched hands once more. 'Good luck for the business trip.'

One week later, in response to a telephone call from Alain, Louise met him for lunch. He looked fit and well and had apparently that day been to see his lawyer. 'The divorce is going through; Hélène has agreed to it after being on her own. At last I can lead the sort of life I've longed for!'

Louise was genuinely happy at his news. 'I can't tell you how glad I am, Alain. Everything will come right for you, I'm sure.'

He gave her an endearing smile that was no longer fixed. 'And you won't agree to giving me the chance to make me the happiest man in the world?'

'I'm sorry, Alain,' Louise said with deep conviction. 'It wouldn't work, I'm afraid. I shall be travelling around for a while, sorting myself out.'

'Like your feelings for Piers?' Alain said quietly. 'Forgive me, Louise, but I think I've known all along. It showed—well, it certainly did to me.'

'I can't deny it, Alain, but I hope that you and I remain good friends for a very long time. All of us, in fact. They're a great team.'

Alain delved into his pocket. 'I almost forgot. Jan and Anna are going away on a prolonged honeymoon; this is their forwarding address. He's so eager that we keep in touch. I think Anna had been playing around while he was away—quite a shock to him, I believe, but they intend giving it another try.' He kissed her when they parted. 'I'll be ever grateful for what you, Jan and Monique did for me, and thanks a million, Louise.' He gave her his temporary address as they said another farewell, and, in a strange sort of way, Louise felt happier that at least there was one person in the world who realised how she felt about Piers, and that she was able to voice it. Maybe there was a lesson there somewhere.

By the following week, Louise was with her parents in the little town of Looe in Cornwall. Once the great excitement of her homecoming had died down, she spent hours walking around the harbour, tramping the long white beaches, handling her parents' boat with its out-board motor on the lazy West Looe River, doing all the things she'd done and loved all her life. She even talked about the jilting rationally with her mother, and it soon became obvious to her concerned parents that she was once more the loving, caring daughter she'd always been, and that the long-drawn-out crisis in her life was over. If her mother had sensed another, more personal abstraction about her, she said nothing, knowing that Louise would deal with it in her own way.

The day before Louise left Cornwall, there was a letter from Monique—it was ecstatic, joyful, happiness pouring from every word.

'Perhaps you will not be surprised to learn that Anjum is coming to Paris on business! He wants us to meet, Louise, and tells me many things I cannot yet believe. . .'

There was that and much more. Dear Monique, Louise thought as she folded the letter away, she deserved every ounce of happiness she could get. Anjum, too. She was still thinking of them while travelling on the Intercity train back to London. Then her parents came to mind, particularly when her father had discussed her future.

'It doesn't matter what you do in the future, my dear, so long as you're happy. If you want to carry on specialising in obstetrics, then do so. I'm sure your old hospital will welcome you.'

In one respect her father turned out to be right. She was offered a job, but only on a temporary basis until the regular houseman returned from sick leave. It might be for one month; no more than three. She accepted the offer, then rang her parents to let them have the address at which she was staying.

It was a dingy bed-sitter in a London street as near the hospital as possible. The rent was exorbitant. For a month she was more miserable than she could imagine. The only thing that seemed to keep her spirits up was the Afghan embroidered mat on the wall—she and Monique had each been given one as a gift by the villagers. The English autumn was already sending out its winter feelers, and she knew very few people at the hospital who had been there in her training days. She hardly went out because of the long and wearying working hours. By November she'd made up her mind to accept a job she'd had offered her in Australia. She still had until December before giving them a final reply. There would be further training, and she fervently believed, as Piers himself had done, that she could be of far more use anywhere else in the world by accepting it.

On a dark afternoon at the hospital, the first snow of the year drifted down against the windowpanes. Trying not to yawn, having been on call the night before, as well as doing an eight-hour stint that day, Louise left the women's ward. She felt heartsick at the empty beds there when patients were counting the days to when they could be operated upon if there were only more staff. The whole situation was crazy. Her bleeper suddenly sprang to life. 'Dr Holden. . . Dr Holden, please. You're wanted in Reception at once. Reception, please. Casualty desperately needs attention. Sorry, no one else on duty available. . .'

Louise took the nearest lift, pushing back her untidy

hair, her white coat flapping round her slim figure, which had refused to put on an extra ounce despite the change of food since Zari. The lift doors opened in Reception, she went to the desk. . .and nearly fainted. Piers stood smiling in front of her, tall, sunburnt, more handsome than ever. She couldn't speak as he apologised, an arm steadying her because she was so unprepared for the ruse which had been played upon her. He had obviously charmed the nurse at the desk to act the part. The sound of his rich, deep voice got through to her.

'Louise, I'm afraid I'm the casualty! I just have to talk to you. I happen to know you live just round the corner.'

Some of the words got through to her. 'What's wrong? What's happened?' she asked anxiously. 'You'd better tell me the symptoms.' She noticed him give a grateful look to the smiling nurse, who was listening with great interest and saying, 'I've ordered your cab, it's here now.'

Louise looked from one to the other, and it suddenly dawned on her. 'Piers Morell, don't play around like this!' she snapped angrily. 'I still have ten more minutes before I'm off duty. I just can't leave. What sort of game is this?'

He took her arm, walking her to where the taxi waited at the kerb. 'Believe me, this is no game!'

In a daze she gave him the address, and within minutes they were in the shamefully furnished little room.

'It's a dump, but temporary, Piers.' She felt unable to think straight. For so long she'd pushed him from her mind, her thoughts, her heart—and now here he was, urging her down into a chair. He had thrown his cashmere overcoat on to the bed, added his suit jacket, then found the kettle and set two mugs on a tray. She watched him, dumbfounded. 'But. . .Piers, what is this all about?'

While waiting for the water to boil he knelt down at the side of her chair. 'I decided when I came back from

Sweden that I could stand this existence no longer. I had to find you, I needed to speak to you, and did so by ringing your father. He very kindly told me where you were. I've come straight from the airport after going to my hotel.' He went to make the tea, then placed the mugs on the floor between them. 'I know I'm taking a calculated risk here, Louise, and I don't care who knows it.' He picked up her mug. 'Drink this first—I can see you're whacked.'

She drank, her hands shaking as she cupped them round the mug. Just the mere sight of Piers had made her act like a congenital idiot. She must pull herself together. 'It's terrific to see you, Piers.' Her eyes filled with stupid tears and she dashed them away quickly. 'I mean, it would have been terrific to see any one of the team, I miss them all so much, particularly here in London. . .' She put the mug aside.

Piers longed to take her in his arms, but he just looked at her, then made up his mind, feeling like a man about to plunge off the Eiffel Tower, hoping to survive. 'Louise—my God, I love you so much. . .have done now for months. I adore you. You have to believe me.' He took her hand and kissed it, encouraged by the way her fingers curled firmly around his. 'I'm sorry if this is all too brusque, or sounds matter-of-fact, but I've been through hell, Louise, and the only thing that's important at the moment is your answer to my question.'

Louise was sure she'd stopped breathing. Her heart had stopped pounding, the world had ceased turning, as dry-lipped she murmured, 'The answer. . .?'

He stood up and drew her to him, holding her close, feasting his eyes on every wonderful plane and contour of her face. 'Louise, will you marry me?'

At his words a million stars exploded around her as she responded with equal brevity, 'Yes, Piers, oh, yes!'

'My wife. . . Thank God!' They kissed then, a perfect symbol of a contract that was to last forever. When they drew apart, they looked like two different people, love

for each other having transformed them. Piers grinned.
'You must think I'm an arrogant devil, taking so much
for granted!'

She kissed his chin. 'I do, but I don't care a jot!'

He looked around the room. 'Come along, my girl—
we're leaving here fast!'

Within half an hour her room was paid off, her luggage
packed, her hospital job ended, and she was in a luxury
hotel with Piers, where he had a double suite. She rang
her parents to tell them the joyous news, saying they
would be in Cornwall shortly before leaving for Paris,
while Piers ordered dinner to be served in their suite.
Once the meal was over, and Louise had overcome the
glorious sight of three dozen red roses being delivered
for her in a presentation basket, they sat together, she
with her head on his shoulder, both talking animatedly
about everything under the sun that concerned them.

'That day in the cave, Piers, when we made love. I
suppose you thought it was. . .just an inevitable
happening?'

'To be honest, perhaps for a time I did; but if I seemed
aloof afterwards, it was because as each day went by I
thought of you more and more. And you?'

'In a sense you gave me back a certain. . .dignity and
pride. From then on I think it was slowly and surely
turning to love. Real love. . .in fact, desperate at times.'

He caught her up in his arms, his kisses convincing
her without any doubt that he felt the same. 'I know for
certain it was getting through that malaria bout, when I
knew just how much you meant to me, darling. I
couldn't tell you. I didn't know enough about you, the
other men in your life—Alain. . .'

Louise shook her head with a smile. 'You were quite
wrong, Piers.' He kissed her then with all the fervour of
the parting they had both endured.

'God, Louise, I've been through hell while I was in
Sweden. So sure I'd found the one person I knew was
for me, and yet not knowing. . .'

'Me too, my love. I was practically on my way to Australia to try and forget! I've been thinking—that malaria incident of yours might not have been such a bad thing after all! It seemed to be the thing that. . .'

'. . .knocked some sense into our heads!'

She glanced at the small scar on his forehead, touching it gently. 'Oh, my poor darling! Thank God you came back for me!'

Piers stood up suddenly. 'I have a small gift for you.' He sat down at her side and handed her a small jewel box. When she opened it, inside lay a gold filigree locket, the size of a plum, and behind the oval glass was the perfect bloom of a blue-mauve clover from the slopes of Afghanistan, beautifully pressed, the locket hanging on its own magnificently wrought chain of gold. She fought back tears.

'Piers, that day in the field of clover. . .'

Lovingly he fastened it around her neck. 'On that day I don't know how I stopped myself from making love to you there and then. I extricated that flower from your hair, and the same night pressed it in my diary. It's since been to a Paris jeweller, and hence the result! That's how much I prayed and hoped things would go right for us, sweetheart.' He smiled, adoring her, the bare, slender throat displaying the first sign of their love to the world. 'Wear it against your heart, my Louise. I insisted the chain be long enough for that purpose. It will serve until we buy your engagement ring, and other things to make up for so much lost time.'

Speechless, Louise clasped the smooth gold oval with its filigree edging in her palm, the feel of it, the true meaning of it bringing a radiance to her face that caught at Piers' throat. They embraced, and time stood still for them.

At length Louise moved slightly from his arms. 'Darling, there's something I must tell you, otherwise it'll grow into greater proportions than it really is.' She saw the sudden anxiety in his eyes, and swiftly told him about Monique and Jan helping Alain out with the operation.

Relief flooded through her when Piers threw back his head and laughed joyfully. 'Oh, Louise, I thought you were going to tell me something devastating!' He led her over to the long windows where London was lit up like fairyland, and the ever-moving traffic a brilliant necklace. 'My darling, the world moves on. That's in the past now, as with so many other things. I have wondered about that, but decided to let it lie. All you and I have to do now is to think of the future. It may be Afghanistan again, who knows? Everything lies ahead. . .after our honeymoon! The future is ours alone. The only casualties we're concerned with at this moment are those of the heart. Love's casualties!' He tilted her chin gently. 'Now, are you going to agree with me for once?'

She gave him a loving smile, her lustrous green eyes twinkling. 'Quite definitely, but after that. . .'

With a low growl he wrapped his arms about her, whispered a few foreign words in her ear, then translated so that they seemed to gravitate naturally to the blue and silver bedroom. Louise ran a hand over his lean jaw, whispering back, 'My Kara Kush!'

Piers' eyes lit up with surprise and delight. 'Sweetheart, this eagle really has found his true mate!' And, very softly, he closed the bedroom door.

DON'T MISS OUT ON HOLIDAY ROMANCE!

Four specially selected brand new novels from popular authors in an attractive easy-to-pack presentation case.

THE TIGER'S LAIR
Helen Bianchin
THE GIRL HE LEFT BEHIND
Emma Goldrick
SPELLBINDING
Charlotte Lamb
FORBIDDEN ATTRACTION
Lilian Peake

This year take your own holiday romance with you.

Look out for the special pack from 29th June, 1990 priced £5.40.

2 COMPELLING READS
FOR AUGUST 1990

HONOUR BOUND – Shirley Larson   £2.99

The last time Shelly Armstrong had seen Justin Corbett, she'd been a tongue tied teenager overwhelmed by his good looks and opulent lifestyle. Now she was an accomplished pilot with her own flying school, and equal to Justin in all respects but one – she was still a novice at loving.

SUMMER LIGHTNING – Sandra James   £2.99

The elemental passions of *Spring Thunder* come alive again in the sequel . . .
Maggie Howard is staunchly against the resumption of logging in her small Oregon town – McBride Lumber had played too often with the lives of families there. So when Jared McBride returned determined to reopen the operation, Maggie was equally determined to block his every move – whatever the cost.

W🌐RLDWIDE

Available from Boots, Martins, John Menzies, W.H. Smith, Woolworths and other paperback stockists.

Zodiac Wordsearch
Competition

How would you like a years supply of Mills & Boon Romances <u>ABSOLUTELY FREE</u>?

Well, you can win them! All you have to do is complete the word puzzle below and send it into us by Dec 31st 1990. The first five correct entries picked out of the bag after this date will each win a years supply of Mills & Boon Romances (Six books every month - worth over £100!) What could be easier?

S	E	C	S	I	P	R	I	A	M	F
I	U	L	C	A	N	C	E	R	L	I
S	A	I	N	I	M	E	G	N	S	R
C	A	P	R	I	C	O	R	N	U	E
S	E	I	R	A	N	G	I	S	I	O
Z	O	D	W	A	T	E	R	B	R	I
O	G	A	H	M	A	T	O	O	A	P
D	R	R	T	O	U	N	I	R	U	R
I	I	B	R	O	R	O	M	G	Q	O
A	V	I	A	N	U	A	N	C	A	C
C	E	L	E	O	S	T	A	R	S	S

Pisces	Aries	Leo	Earth
Cancer	Gemini	Virgo	Star
Scorpio	Taurus	Fire	Sign
Aquarius	Libra	Water	Moon
Capricorn	Sagittarius	Zodiac	Air

Please turn over for entry details

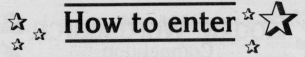

☆ How to enter ☆

All the words listed overleaf, below the word puzzle, are hidden
in the grid. You can can find them by reading the letters
forwards, backwards, up and down, or diagonally. When you find
a word, circle it, or put a line through it. After you have found all
the words, the left-over letters will spell a secret message that
you can read from left to right, from the top of the puzzle
through to the bottom.

Don't forget to fill in your name and address in the space provided
and pop this page in an envelope (you don't need a stamp) and
post it today.   Competition closes Dec 31st 1990.

Only one entry
per household
(more than one
will render the
entry invalid).

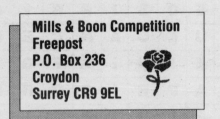

Mills & Boon Competition
Freepost
P.O. Box 236
Croydon
Surrey CR9 9EL

Hidden message _____

_____

Are you a Reader Service subscriber.   Yes ☐   No ☐

Name_____

Address_____

_____

_____

_____ **Postcode**_____

COMP9